insight text guide

Robert Beardwood & Kate Macdonell

Minimum of Two

Tim Winton

First published in 2004, reprinted with revisions in 2013, 2015, 2017, 2020, 2021.

Insight Publications Pty Ltd
3/350 Charman Road
Cheltenham VIC 3192
Australia
Tel: +61 3 8571 4950
Fax: +61 3 8571 0257
Email: books@insightpublications.com.au

www.insightpublications.com.au

National Library of Australia Cataloguing-in-Publication entry:
Beardwood, Robert, 1966-.
Insight text guide: Minimum of Two – Tim Winton.
ISBN 9781920693589
1. Winton, Tim, 1960-. Minimum of Two. I. Macdonell, Kate, 1969-.
II. Title. (Series: Insight text guide).
A823.3

Other ISBNs:
9781922378873 (digital)
9781922378880 (bundle: print + digital)

Cover design: The Modern Art Production Group

Printed in Australia.

contents

CHARACTER TABLES

Table 1: Central male characters and their relationships

Central Male Character	Stories	Major Relationship	Significant Others	Relationship with Father/Parents
Jerra Nilsam	'Forest Winter', 'Gravity', 'Nilsam's Friend', 'Bay of Angels', 'More', 'Blood and Water'	Rachel Nilsam – wife	Sam – son	Mostly positive: father dies, and in 'Gravity' is missed
'The boy'	'No Memory Comes'	The boy's friend	The friend's girlfriend	Father leaves
Madigan	'Minimum of Two'	Greta – wife	Fred Blakey – Greta's rapist	Unknown
Hart	'Holding'	Clive Genders – friend	Jan Genders – Clive's wife	Unknown
'The Man'	'Death Belongs To The Dead'	'the Dying Gentleman' – customer	None	Remembers father's advice

Table 2: Central female characters and their relationships

Central Female Character	Story	Major Relationship	Significant Others	Relationship with Father/Parents
Rachel Nilsam	'The Strong One'	Jerra – husband	Sam – son	Negative; parents absent
Queenie Cookson	'Laps'	Cleve Cookson – husband	Dot – daughter	Misses grandfather
Fat Maz	'Distant Lands'	None	The 'dark man' who reads *Distant Lands*	Not close
'The girl'	'The Water Was Dark'	Mother	None	Father absent; mother's negativity resented

INTRODUCTION

Tim Winton is one of Australia's most popular and critically acclaimed authors. These fourteen stories, first published in the 1980s, show Winton in an early, formative phase, deploying a terse, minimalist prose style that occasionally bursts into more lyrical and reflective passages. As always in Winton's fiction, these stories display a profound and compassionate concern for ordinary people who struggle to meet the challenges of everyday life and to negotiate the occasional traumatic episode that leaves lasting scars on the psyche.

Minimum of Two reflects the changing nature of Australian society during the 1980s, a period when an increasing divorce rate and new flexibility in gender roles meant family and work patterns had to be freshly negotiated. Yet the stories also explore questions of timeless significance: about the beginning and ending of life, and about the nature of happiness and contentment.

Spanning the collection are seven stories about Jerra and Rachel Nilsam, a young married couple who struggle to raise a child with little in the way of material or educational resources behind them. Interspersed with the Nilsams' stories are seven about a variety of other characters. Some are children and adolescents, some in mid-life and some nearing the end of life. Irrespective of their life stages, they are linked by their experiences of loss and by the difficulty encountered by each of them of achieving lasting intimacy.

The degree to which the characters succeed in responding to these challenges varies considerably. At times it seems as though they are subject to forces beyond their control – a breech birth, a terminal illness, a father who leaves suddenly and irrevocably. At other times, characters yearn for something lost and risk all that they have for what no longer exists.

Note: for simplicity, the titles of two stories are abbreviated in this text guide. 'The Water Was Dark And It Went Forever Down' is shortened to 'The Water Was Dark...'; and 'Death Belongs To The Dead, His Father Told Him, And Sadness To The Sad' is shortened to 'Death Belongs To The Dead...'.

What unites Winton's characters is their common humanity. And sometimes too there is an uncertain glimpse of the possibility that there is something 'more' to life beyond the mundane here-and-now. For all its grim desperation, there is a hint of beneficence in Winton's fictional worlds, a touch of grace that relieves the arduousness of existence and makes love, as fragile as it is, actually possible.

BACKGROUND & CONTEXT

Background: Tim Winton and his fiction

Tim Winton was born in Perth in 1960 and spent much of his childhood in Perth and the south-coast town of Albany. After leaving school Winton studied creative writing at the Western Australian Institute of Technology (now Curtin University). Winton's first two novels, *An Open Swimmer* (1982) and *Shallows* (1984), were published when he was in his early twenties and both won major literary awards.

From this auspicious beginning, Winton's writing has continued to receive a high level of critical and popular acclaim. The novels *Breath* (2008) and *Dirt Music* (2001) both won the Miles Franklin Literary Award. Other novels that have won the praise and affection of many readers include *Cloudstreet* (1991), which has also been turned into an internationally successful stage play and a television miniseries, and *The Riders* (1994), which was shortlisted for the 1995 Booker Prize. In addition to these literary works, Winton has also published the Lockie Leonard series of books for children.

Links between Winton's novels and *Minimum of Two*

Winton's first two novels have some interesting connections with the stories in *Minimum of Two*. The two central characters of 'Laps', Queenie and Cleve Cookson, look back on traumatic events that took place when they lived in Angelus, events that are dramatically narrated in *Shallows*. The character Jerra Nilsam, who features in several stories in *Minimum of Two*, is also the protagonist of *An Open Swimmer*. The novel is set earlier than the stories and centres on the friendship between Jerra and Sean. In 'The Strong One', Jerra fondly recalls camping with Sean and then is shocked to learn of Sean's death. However, the friendship as portrayed in *An Open Swimmer* is more fraught than Jerra's affectionate memories in 'The Strong One' suggest.

Changing gender roles and family structures

Unlike some Australian novelists whose work has concentrated on historical settings – Peter Carey's *True History of the Kelly Gang* (1999) is a good example – Winton has been concerned mostly with issues directly pertaining to his own time and place. One social issue that became more important during the 1980s (when these stories were first published) was the changing nature of family relationships, due both to new attitudes towards gender roles and to the increasing divorce rate. The historically conventional allocation of responsibilities within the family unit, with the father earning all or most of the family's income and the mother performing most domestic and child-rearing duties, continued to be regarded as 'normal'. However, this structure was gradually modified in more and more families during the 1970s and 1980s.

In 'The Strong One', Rachel Nilsam asserts her right to a university education and suggests that Jerra can look after their son, Sam. Jerra admits to being 'scared' that he 'won't be able to do it properly', to which Rachel retorts: 'How do you think I felt?' (p.100). The notions that women are equally entitled to a profession, and are not innately suited to raising children any more than men are, were not new in Australian literature in 1987. The seminal feminist novels *My Brilliant Career* by Miles Franklin (1901) and *The Getting of Wisdom* by Henry Handel Richardson[1] (1910) express precisely these sentiments. Nevertheless, by the late 1980s Rachel's affirmative attitude towards the equality and negotiable nature of gender roles was more widely accepted in Australian society than it ever had been previously.

Winton's Western Australian settings

Tim Winton has lived almost all of his life in south-west Western Australia, and the distinctive history and natural features of that area provide the settings for most of his fiction, including *Minimum of Two*. In stories that

[1] This is a pseudonym; the author's real name was Ethel Florence Lindesay Richardson.

explore universal human experiences – such as birth, death, feelings of alienation and loss – specific settings are less important. Yet even in these narratives a Western Australian setting is usually indicated, often by a place name such as (Perth's) Kings Park in 'Bay of Angels', Fremantle in 'Minimum of Two' or Bridgetown in 'Forest Winter'.

Alternatively, the narrative sometimes refers to a distinctively Western Australian aspect of the natural environment, like the Karri forests in 'Forest Winter'. Another wood closely identified with Western Australia is jarrah; Blakey's former house in 'Minimum of Two' has 'big jarrah doors' (p.53), for instance. In 'Gravity', Rachel's tanned skin 'made her look as though she was made from polished jarrah' (p.27), which suggests there is a strong connection between Rachel and the Western Australian environment. The similarity of the names 'Jerra' and 'jarrah' has the same effect.

In other stories, Winton draws his local knowledge more directly into the narrative. Winton lived for a number of years in Albany, which had an important whaling industry from the nineteenth century until the late 1970s, when the Fraser government legislated to end whaling in Australia. In 'Laps', the 'awesome cliffs and beaches' of the southern coastline establish the physical landscape (p.79), and the transition of the whaling industry through protest movements towards tourism forms the cultural and historical backdrop to the story.

The role and value of the coast

Winton has lived mostly on or near the coast, and his affection for beaches, bays and rivers is reflected in the many such settings in *Minimum of Two*. Recently, the value that Winton attaches to the coast has found a more overtly political expression in the community-based campaign to stop the development of Ningaloo Reef in Western Australia. Winton's involvement in the campaign has been motivated by an appreciation of the intrinsic value of the coastline and its potential for a sustainable ecotourism industry. He has also been moved by anger and regret about the development of the Scarborough beachfront in the late 1980s:

> I grew up in the beachside suburb of Scarborough, a community intimately connected with the sea. As a young man I watched as a starstruck Labor government let Alan Bond build his trophy tower on our beachfront where high-rise was outlawed…the 20-storey luxury hotel that isolated us from the sea and ate up the modest shops and apartments that had been our neighbourhood.[2]

This mixture of disbelief and dismay about coastal development also finds expression in two stories in *Minimum of Two*. In 'No Memory Comes', the boy sees the signs of the development on an unnamed beachfront but 'doesn't believe it will happen' (p.17). The story expresses a sense of loss with regard to the demolished 'burger joints and pinball parlours' and a rejection of the 'ugly bones of the hotel tower' (p.17).

In 'Laps' the same scenario is located explicitly in Scarborough, where 'little men with big money were tearing up the beachfront to build hotels' (p.76). Again, the loss of the older businesses and lifestyles that seemed more attuned to the landscape is registered with a tone of pathos; their absence leaves an 'awful wound in the ground where the burger joints and pinball parlours had been' (p.76).

---

[2] Tim Winton, 'Our reef, my belief', *The Weekend Australian* 30 Nov–1 Dec 2002, p.21.

GENRE, STRUCTURE & STYLE

The arrangement of stories

The order of the fourteen stories in the collection has a particular effect on the way in which the stories are read – assuming the reader proceeds from first page to last. The seven stories concerning Jerra and Rachel Nilsam are evenly distributed, mostly being separated by one story about unrelated characters. These various characters are at different life stages from one another but they often face similar difficulties. The juxtaposition of certain stories encourages the observation of links between them, such as:

- in the second, third and fourth stories, characters experience or remember the loss of their father
- 'More' and the following story, 'Death Belongs to the Dead...', have characters with terminal illnesses
- water settings and images of swimming link 'Laps' and 'Bay of Angels'.

Jerra and Rachel: stories that span the collection

The stories about Rachel and Jerra Nilsam span the collection, including its opening and closing stories. The vicissitudes of their lives invest the collection with much of its dramatic tension and coherence. One or both of Jerra and Rachel appear in 'Forest Winter', 'Gravity', 'Nilsam's Friend', 'Bay of Angels' (Jerra is identified by his reference to his son, Sam), 'The Strong One', 'More' and 'Blood and Water'.

These stories chart a period of transition in Rachel and Jerra's lives, from the end of a time of optimism and of Jerra's time with his band – 'cruising up and down the coast in a Kombi' as Rachel recalls it (p.100) – to the beginning of a new phase, settled in a Perth suburb. During these years they experience the traumatic birth of their son, Sam; the death of Jerra's father, Tom; the constant stress of an uncertain and limited income; and the changes that come with Rachel studying at university, including Jerra taking over the primary parenting responsibilities.

Interestingly, the order of these stories in the collection does not strictly follow the chronology of Jerra and Rachel's lives. 'Blood and Water', the story of Sam's birth which concludes the collection, has the earliest setting. 'Forest Winter', which opens the volume, is set nine weeks later, during the Nilsams' bleak sojourn in the country. In 'Gravity', one of the latest in setting, Sam is three years old and Rachel is establishing herself in social work.

Thus, questions raised in such stories as 'Forest Winter' and 'The Strong One' about the circumstances of Sam's birth are only answered in the final story, allowing the reader's curiosity to build progressively. Similarly, the nature of Jerra's relationship with his father, crucial to his memories and feelings in 'Gravity', is explored in 'More', set earlier than 'Gravity' but placed later in the collection.

How the stories are structured

The stories range in length from brief sketches of a few pages to longer, more complexly plotted stories of around ten pages. The shorter stories, such as 'Bay of Angels', 'Nilsam's Friend' and 'The Water Was Dark...', cover a brief period of time and involve only one or two characters. The interest in these stories is less in a sequence of events than in the evocation of a strong mood or feeling – of anger, in the case of the girl in 'The Water Was Dark...', or of sadness in 'Bay of Angels'. No sooner is the scene set than the story concludes, without the tension implicit in the situation being resolved.

In the longer stories, the narrative tension is sustained and developed toward a climax, such as Madigan's assault of Blakey and his girlfriend in 'Minimum of Two' or Sam's birth and first breath in 'Blood and Water'. Even in these more conventionally structured stories, though, Winton typically ends on a note of ambiguity. 'More' is a good example: although Jerra and Rachel are partially reconciled at the end, their attempt to kiss is interrupted by the sudden flight of quail from the undergrowth. The story concludes with Jerra hearing 'the blood beating at his throat' (p.131), fearful rather than reassured.

Key point

In the traditional form of the short story, tensions and conflicts are neatly resolved. However, Winton manipulates this structure to suggest that tension in people's lives does not necessarily disappear, but often must simply be accepted in an ongoing struggle for survival and contentment.

Style: things that remain unsaid

Winton's style in *Minimum of Two* tends to be minimalist, and there are two main ways in which this style is thematically significant. Firstly, it reflects Winton's interest in ordinary people who are not well educated, not wealthy and not working in white-collar professions. They are not completely inarticulate, but nor do they use a sophisticated vocabulary or express themselves with great fluency.

Winton's interest in ordinary people is also reflected in the absence of character names. In some stories, the narrative refers to characters by such generic labels as 'the boy', 'the girl', 'The Man' and 'the Dying Gentleman'. This gives the stories a folkloric quality. The narrative focus is less on the individual and more on the universal dimensions of their experience, such as an encounter with death, an adolescence filled with fear and anger, or simply a struggle to complete a day's work.

Secondly, Winton's minimalist prose style understates or conceals details of the characters' thoughts and feelings. For instance, the boy in 'No Memory Comes' remembers 'a mob of things' (p.18) but, rather than describe the memories, the narrative simply gives the words to the song that triggers them. This withholding of details reflects the reluctance of characters to talk about, or even acknowledge to themselves, their true circumstances. It also heightens the sense of distance between reader and character, forcing the reader to guess at a character's deeper reasons for acting in a certain way and thereby mimicking the emotional distance between many of the characters.

Style: poetic qualities in water imagery

Offsetting the minimalist aspects of Winton's prose style is a more poetic and expansive quality evident in descriptions of water. Although Winton tends to use adjectives sparingly, when evoking images of water he uses adjectives in strings, as in 'clean, shallow water' or 'shifting filter of river water' (p.121, 'More'). The phrase 'tide-ribbed bottom' (p.121) uses the poetic device of alliteration – in the repeated 'b' and 'd' – and thus captures the gentle pulsing rhythm of the waves. These techniques allow the narrative to gain a more lyrical tone, reflecting the possibilities for contemplation or appreciating beauty that bodies of water provide in these stories.

STORY-BY-STORY ANALYSIS

The significance of the epigraph

Following the book's dedication 'to Jesse and Denise' (Winton's son and wife) is an epigraph, which comprises three lines of a playground chant:

> One and one make one
> and one
> and one and one make one...

This epigraph points to some of the central preoccupations of the stories. Firstly, it foregrounds their interest in childhood as a unique time of innocence and play, yet also of vulnerability. Secondly, the epigraph highlights the connected issues of relationships and isolation through the contradiction of adding 'one and one' but only ending up with one rather than two. This theme is played out in the stories through their depictions of people struggling to form relationships or families – in other words, to form a 'minimum of two'. Even when Winton's characters come together as friends or as partners they often feel isolated from one another.

'Forest Winter' (pp.1–9)

Summary: *Jerra chops wood in the country and Rachel recovers from Sam's birth; Rachel has a near-fatal asthma attack; the old Ventolin canister explodes in the fire, temporarily blinding Jerra.*

This story introduces the reader to Jerra Nilsam; his wife, Rachel; and their son, Sam (referred to as 'the baby' in this story). 'Forest Winter' shows Jerra and Rachel's responses to crises that are compounded by their poverty and their isolation in the country.

Hard times

Two crises occur in 'Forest Winter'. The first is Rachel's life-threatening asthma attack, a result of her Ventolin being too old to use. The second and related crisis occurs when the old Ventolin container that Jerra has put carelessly into the firebox explodes in his face. The explosion temporarily blinds Jerra but he soon recovers his sight. Both incidents partly derive from poverty as well as unthinking behaviour, reflecting Winton's concern with the limitations and vulnerable qualities of adult life.

The 'man on the land'

Jerra Nilsam had previously worked as a musician but now he and his family have moved to the country in an effort to find respite from the dole and to seek a better lifestyle. However, their situation is bleak and Jerra laments that 'the music was gone, the money. And Rachel, what had happened to her?' (p.5). That Jerra is chopping up trees that have already *fallen* and that at times he is almost 'catatonic from misery' (p.3) signposts Winton's interest in less heroic models of Australian masculinity.

Key point

'Forest Winter' places pressure on the stereotype of the Australian man on the land as someone who is rugged and self-sufficient. The narrative's reference to Jerra as 'the young man' – only revealing his name towards the end of the story – suggests that his psychological isolation reflects a general experience.

Jerra drives Rachel to Bridgetown rather than seeking help from his employer who lives close by. This unwillingness to seek help from his boss, and Jerra's sense that the pharmacist will not be of assistance because 'he thinks I'm a junkie' (p.6), highlight Jerra's sense of isolation and his cynicism towards an ethos of mateship.

The indifference of nature

The natural world offers little solace for Jerra and his family. However, at times there is a synergy between natural and human entities. People can take on attributes of the weather or trees; for instance, Sam's cry is a 'squall' (p.4), and Rachel's raspy breath sounds like 'a bough breaking loose in a storm' (p.4). Likewise, trees take on human characteristics when they are described as being subject to 'dismembering' (p.3) or as 'bodies of trees' (p.5). In this scenario, human individuals are not nurtured or uplifted by the natural world, but nor are they alienated from it.

Images of nature reflect Jerra's isolation and melancholic frame of mind. The sound of magpies is 'misanthropic' (p.4), the wind is 'hard and cold' (p.3) and the clouds form a 'maelstrom' (p.7). The rain 'trickling down the windows' of Jerra's utility (p.3) figuratively embodies his despair, as if the natural world can mimic his emotional state but not improve it.

Q What is the significance of the song Jerra sings to Sam, 'A frog went walking on a summer's day'?

Q Does the story suggest that the Nilsams' crises result from the workings of fate and chance, or from their own actions?

'No Memory Comes' (pp.11–21)

Summary: *A boy's father abandons his family to be with his housegirl in Hong Kong; the boy's relationship with his best friend changes as they grow up but he refuses to recognise change.*

I: New Year's Eve

The story opens on New Year's Eve, a time when many people look forward to new beginnings. However, for 'the boy' – who remains unnamed throughout – familiar things are sufficient. When he accidentally disturbs two strangers having sex on a beach, he rushes back to his parents. Later he falls asleep in their bed, hoping that 'the new year will never come' (p.13).

II: The actions of men

That catastrophic changes can happen in life is clear when the boy and his friend discover the body of a man who has committed suicide. The boy's friend cries, revealing that he 'wets the bed every night' (p.14) and that his father once made him go to school with his wet pyjamas wrapped around his neck as a punishment.

III: Philosophical dilemmas

The two friends wonder what will happen when the world ends – foregrounding their naive curiosity about the future. The boy has a strong belief in life's ritual and continuity. This is reinforced by his knowledge that the beach he goes to was also frequented by his mother when she was younger. The beach setting also symbolically evokes these links between past, present and future: the beach is an in-between (or liminal) zone, where the tides of life roll on and away.

IV: Changes

This section is the mid-point of the story and a turning point in the boy's life. The boy's father decides to remain in Hong Kong with his housegirl-lover. The boy cries and beats his knuckles against the bathroom tiles. This is the last display of emotion we see from him; significantly, he endeavours to keep it private by locking the door and turning on the shower.

The father's betrayal not only destroys the family unit, but also changes the way the boy views the world. No longer does he think of the future; rather, the past – a time before sex and the complexities of relationships impacted on his life – now becomes his obsession.

V: Living in the past

The boy talks incessantly about the past, keeps his hair long and dresses unfashionably (p.16). While the boy occupies the margins of the peer group, his friend is at its centre. When the boy and his friend are sixteen they buy a car together, but then the friend 'keeps the car at his own place' (p.17). When the friend's girlfriend drives around with them the boy is relegated to the back seat, even suffering the embarrassment of being present when the friend and the girl have sex.

Key point

Even though the boy swears that things are 'the same' (pp.16–17), he is clearly deluding himself. The boy's desire for things not to change now becomes an act of denial that change has already occurred.

VI: A hole inside

The boy finishes his final exams but 'feels a hole open in him' (p.17), a feeling of loss and emptiness associated with the ending of childhood without hope for the future. He describes going prawning with his father, showing how he continues to take refuge imaginatively in the past.

At the beach house the boy confronts the past yet finds he is unable to feel anything in response to it. He attempts to open an old beer can with an instrument that 'looks like a scythe' (p.20). The blade slips and he accidentally stabs himself in the groin. If the boy's attempt to access the contents of the can is interpreted as an attempt to salvage something useful or positive from the past, then the boy's injury is a metaphor for how self-destructive this obsession with the past can be.

VII: Remembering / dismembering

In the immediate aftermath of the accident, no memory comes to the boy's mind. On one level he feels the wind lashing his body, the blood heating his pants and the motor throbbing in his ears. Yet on another level the boy is now without feeling, as if completely disconnected not merely from the past but from his own life.

Q How are sexual relationships represented in this story?

Q How does the narrative represent women and men? Is one gender represented more positively than the other?

'Gravity' (pp.23–32)

Summary: *On the anniversary of his father's death, Jerra struggles to come to terms with his loss, causing tensions as he and Rachel host a birthday party for a friend.*

Set in 1985, 'Gravity' continues the story of the Nilsam family a few years after the events of 'Forest Winter'. The story focuses on Jerra's sense of loss on the anniversary of his father's death, and derives its tension from Jerra's feeling that family and the 'gravity' of memory matter more than social commitments to friends.

The ruined party

Jerra and Rachel are hosting a birthday party for their friend Ann, but Jerra is reluctant to return home from the city café where he and Sam spend the afternoon. Jerra has been 'afraid' (p.25) of the day's emotional significance since waking. Eventually, Jerra straps Sam, who is now three years old, onto the bike and they cycle home. Rachel confronts Jerra about not having done anything for the party and she begins to cry. Her crying 'always frightened' Jerra (p.27), suggesting that it is people's emotions – including his own – of which Jerra is most afraid.

Philip, Ann's husband and a friend of Jerra's, tells him that Ann is 'offended' (p.27), but Jerra is unable to respond sensitively to Philip or to any of the other social worker guests whose conversations Jerra dismisses as 'bloody Deep and Meaningfuls' (p.28). However, the narrative tone suggests that Jerra's reflection that 'It's a party, for God's sake' (p.28) is disingenuous; he is certainly in no mood for partying himself.

Family, loss and memory

During the day Jerra feels an unresolved sense of loss, as if there is 'a hole in him' and there is 'nothing for Jerra Nilsam to fall against' (p.29). He remembers that the bicycle ride home with Sam had a sense of 'gravity' rather than 'exhilaration' (p.29). This is the only use of the word that gives the story its title, but its connotations of seriousness and heaviness run through the descriptions of Jerra's emotional state.

In a dream, Jerra remembers being given a bike one Christmas and his father teaching him to ride it. The way he imaginatively relives the lesson, however, suggests that its real significance relates to Jerra's current difficulty in coping with his father's death. Jerra thinks of his father as the '*Old man holding the back of the seat*' (p.30). Then, when Jerra's father lets go of the bike, Jerra experiences a '*sudden grave feeling of independence*' (p.30), reflecting Jerra's current anxiety due to the permanent loss of his father.

Blood and water

Jerra's music studio is an important space in this story because his father built it shortly before he died. Jerra recalls his father calling the studio 'his Ark' (p.31); that is, it is a place of refuge from the world, and also a means of reaching into the future, a gift to a younger generation. The reference to cancer as an illness that turns 'blood...to water' (p.31) evokes the saying 'blood is thicker than water', and thus underscores the narrative's investment in the value of family relationships.

Key point

Although Jerra's father is no longer alive, his blood continues to circulate (metaphorically) in his descendents, Jerra and Sam. The significance of this notion as a source of continuity and meaning in people's lives is reinforced by Winton's dedication of the stories to his own wife and son as 'my blood, my water', and by the story about Sam's birth being titled 'Blood and Water'.

It is this notion of continuity, the way that families reach not just back into the past but out into the future, that leads to a restoration of Jerra's sense of wellbeing. He realises the value inherent in family relationships, not just the one he had with his father but also those he has with Rachel and Sam, which collectively are inseparable from his own identity: 'Nilsam was a father. He was a husband. He was a son' (p.31). Later that night, feeling far more at peace, he takes Sam to the toilet, grins at the '*homely*, ammoniac smell' (p.32, emphasis added) and resolves to visit his mother on the following day.

Q Rachel is likened to both 'polished jarrah' (p.27) and 'mahogany' (p.28). What do these descriptors connote about her body, her personality and her relationship with her husband?

Q Jerra's father described the studio as his 'Ark', whereas Rachel refers to it as 'the Tower of Babel' (p.31). What do these two biblical allusions suggest about the two characters and their attitudes towards Jerra's musical pursuits?

'The Water Was Dark And It Went Forever Down' (pp.33–9)

Summary: *A fourteen-year-old girl who has lost her father and has a difficult relationship with her mother swims to a small island.*

This story centres on a mother-daughter relationship, contrasting with the interest of 'Gravity' in father-son relationships. Like the protagonist of 'No

Memory Comes', the girl is simply called 'the girl' and she suffers from the childhood experience of losing her father. Although the implication is that the father abandoned his family, the expression 'her father had been gone a year' (p.35) suppresses the details, reflecting the girl's tendency to repress her feelings. Her mother's anger towards men, evident in statements such as *'Men hate us'* and *'Your father never loved you'* (p.36), reinforces the impression that the father left voluntarily.

One reason that the girl's mother is so reclusive is that she was badly burned in a fire caused when she fell asleep while smoking. That she chose to wait until morning before calling an ambulance, rather than waking her daughter, suggests that her self-esteem was extremely low. However, the girl is unable to see her mother's position sympathetically and thinks of her as 'either stupid or sick' (p.35).

Survival tactics: the web of life

The girl does not reflect on her own feelings towards her father even though at five years of age she would have been old enough to have had a meaningful relationship with him. Her emotional coldness suggests that, even though she appears unsympathetic to her mother's unhappiness, she too has been affected by her father's departure.

The girl swims to an island that is full of birds 'hatching, growing, hunting, mating, dying' (p.38). There are also many dead birds on the island. The girl conceptualises what she sees in terms of the 'web of life' she has learnt about at school: 'the sick and the weak died and the young and the strong lived and thrived' (p.38). Clearly she views herself as someone who is 'fit' to survive in a way that her mother is not. This view underscores the girl's tendency to suppress emotional complexities in favour of more simplistic formulations.

The idea of a 'web of life' intersects with another meaning of 'the web' – a spider's web, suggesting entrapment. With greater urgency, the girl swims back towards the shore, trying not to think or to feel anger: 'I can be a machine... I can swim away' (p.39). However, the end of the story suggests that her sense of freedom and independence is illusory.

An ambiguous ending

The narrative is ambiguous about whether or not the girl returns to the shore. The meaning of the phrase 'all the way down', especially following the sentence 'But she faltered' (p.39), is by no means clear. It could refer to the girl's movement down through the channel; it could refer to her psyche; it could refer to her passage towards the bottom of the ocean. Regardless of which interpretation you agree with, the ambiguity of the ending undermines the simplicity of the girl's sense that being 'young and strong and perfect' (p.39) is all that matters in life. The narrative itself has a more sophisticated take on life, encompassing the inescapable complexities of emotions and familial relationships.

Q How does the narrative place pressure on the girl's opinion that: 'Live. Survive. They're the same thing' (p.38)? Describe the difference between 'survival' and 'life' as they are represented in the story.

'Nilsam's Friend' (pp.41–6)

Summary: *Jerra's friend, who has been travelling in Europe, returns unexpectedly.*

The appearance of Jerra's (unnamed) friend, bearded, barefoot and thin, immediately suggests that he is outside the social mainstream. As Jerra looks through the window, his friend appears 'distorted in the gentle convexities of the leadlight' (p.43). Jerra sees his friend as someone difficult to pin down, someone capable of providing 'atmosphere by the suitcase' (p.44) but never anything more concrete. The intention of the friend's trip had been to help him 'get his head together' (p.43) and decide whether or not to marry his girlfriend. By the end of the story, though, it is clear that Jerra's friend has no desire to make this kind of commitment.

A world of difference

The recent experiences of Nilsam's friend are antithetical to Jerra's life in suburban Perth. As Jerra listens, he feels both anxious about and contented with his own life. The narrative's juxtaposition of Jerra's responsibilities (as Sam's primary carer) with his friend's apparent lack of responsibilities is consolidated by Jerra's sense of their physical and intellectual differences. Jerra feels 'overweight, sluggish, ignorant', the opposite of the 'hard and wiry' look of his friend (p.44) and the basis of a slight envy of his friend's lifestyle.

The suburban ordinary

Jerra's joke about having the 'Biggest rooster in the world' is not simply a humorous parody of a little girl's statement that 'Bach was the greatest composer in the world. So was Handel' (p.45). It also reflects Jerra's understanding of his own experiences as suburban and 'ordinary', not pretentious or elitist.

In contrast to his frame of mind in 'Forest Winter' and 'Gravity', here Jerra clearly derives contentment from watching Sam determinedly climb the steps and waiting for Rachel to return from work. He does wonder about seeing 'the same creamy light' of Perth (p.45) in another part of the world. However, his friend's visit prompts Jerra to consider the rewards of his own life as a father and husband, and the story reflects Jerra's growing ease with the choices he has made.

Q What does Jerra's feeling of being 'dowdy like women were supposed to feel dowdy' (p.45) suggest about his level of contentment and his understanding of gender roles?

Q What is the significance of the image of the suburb's 'close-set houses and smudges of smoke from the spring burn-off' (p.45)? Are its connotations positive or negative – or partly both?

'Minimum of Two' (pp.47–63)

Summary: *Neil Madigan's wife, Greta, is raped by her boss, Fred Blakey; Blakey is imprisoned for a 'minimum of two' years; Madigan's relationship with Greta deteriorates; when Blakey is released, Madigan follows him and then runs over Blakey and his girlfriend.*

The confronting introduction to this story immediately establishes a high level of narrative tension. Neil Madigan, the story's first-person narrator, describes his attempt to have sex with his wife as she sleeps. He acts in this way partly because he loves Greta, but also because of his frustration at the lack of intimacy in their relationship. Since Greta was raped by Fred Blakey, a senior work colleague, her relationship with Madigan has deteriorated to the point where Madigan is now virtually willing to rape her himself.

The madness of Madigan

Greta awakes and forces Madigan off her; he retreats to his workshop and reflects on how his marriage has changed. Initially Greta did not tell Madigan about being raped but he 'forced it out of her' (p.50). This expression, combined with Madigan's attempt to force himself on Greta, indicates that Madigan tends to respond aggressively to emotional difficulties. Madigan's name sounds like 'mad again', suggesting that reason and calmness do not come naturally to him. When Greta no longer wishes to have sex with him, Madigan is unable to discuss the situation and ends up 'going mad out in the workshop' (p.52).

Madigan displays no capacity or inclination to think about Greta's psychological state; he 'knew she needed time' (p.52) but otherwise his knowledge of her thoughts and feelings seems nonexistent. His assertion that Greta 'never remembered dreams' (p.52) completely discounts the possibility that she simply does not want to reveal her dreams to him. Madigan thinks not of what Greta has lost but of his own lack, especially of sexual activity: his 'body began to feel as though something had been hacked out of it' (p.57). It is this feeling of loss that Madigan imagines he can restore to a sense of wholeness by murdering Fred Blakey.

Murdering Fred Blakey

The narrative takes on the form of a thriller once Madigan decides to kill Fred Blakey. The irrationality of this decision is evident even to Madigan, who admits that his 'brain seemed a step behind every action' (p.53). This disjunction between thought and action lends a dreamlike quality to the narrative; unlikely events follow one after the other and Madigan is caught up uncomprehendingly in the momentum of his own fantasies.

Compounding Madigan's anger towards Blakey for destroying his marriage is his increasing jealousy of Blakey's lifestyle. Madigan visits Blakey's house in a suburb where 'everything stinks of new money' (p.53), then discovers that Blakey has not suffered greatly during his time in prison. Madigan is shocked when he discovers that Blakey has a girlfriend who 'didn't look twenty years old' (p.61). She picks up Blakey from Fremantle Gaol and they drive to a house in the same exclusive suburb Blakey had lived in previously, a house Madigan thinks makes his own 'look quaint' (p.61).

Madigan's jealousy increases still further when he secretly watches Blakey and the girl having sex. Madigan is incredulous that Blakey, just 'twelve hours out of a gaol' (p.62), has everything Madigan himself yearns for. Madigan is tortured by the image of Blakey's 'heaving white back on Greta' (p.62), and by the idea that Blakey has not only marked and defiled Greta's body – she has a persistent rash on her chest – but also has stained Madigan with 'his big white body' (p.62).

For a moment it seems as if Madigan might change his mind about murdering Blakey. After sleeping through the early hours of the morning in his hired car he wakes and 'felt sad' (p.62). However, Madigan's 'mind was bogged' (p.63) and events continue to unfold in a dreamlike and occasionally cinematic fashion. When Madigan's car hits Blakey, the body moves as if in slow motion: it 'starwheeled up over the bonnet' (p.63). There is no description of the wounded or murdered bodies, only an observation of the 'mist on the river' (p.63) like a still frame in a movie. Only when Madigan returns home and tries to reassure Greta that things are 'all right' does he realise that his crime has effectively made him 'a dead man' (p.63).

Q What does Madigan's admission that he and Greta used to 'slip [china] into handbags when things were tougher' (p.58) tell you about the social class they belong to?

'Distant Lands' (pp.65–71)

Summary: *A girl known as 'Fat Maz' allows a man to read a paperback novel called Distant Lands during lunch hours in her parents' newsagency; when he finishes, he gives her fifty dollars 'for the bus'.*

'Distant Lands' features an enigmatic central character, a girl called Fat Maz who is caught in-between childhood and adulthood. Like the teenagers in 'No Memory Comes' and 'The Water Was Dark...', Fat Maz is an outsider; she is 'not a sporty girl' (p.68) and 'had no friends' (p.70). Nor is she close to her parents. At work she is mostly described looking after the newsagency on her own during her parents' lunch hour. Even when her parents are present they do not communicate or interact with her.

Isolation and apathy

The girl's social isolation is heightened by her sense of remoteness, reflected in the fact that the bus to the city, the 'big Greyhound' (p.67), only goes once each day. In fact, the bus is described as 'pulling away empty' (p.70), suggesting that the town's inhabitants have limited curiosity about the rest of the world. The girl rides her bicycle 'to the edge of town' to 'look along the highway' (p.68) – to see, that is, that there might be more to her life, without being tempted to explore beyond the world she knows too well.

Fat Maz's parents perform their work with a mixture of apathy and resentment. Her father 'clomped up and down' while her mother 'sat all day at the register and watched the cars pass' (p.67). They are partially trapped by their situation, but they are in a kind of stupor, too, disinclined to improve their circumstances.

Imagining escape

Each lunch hour, Fat Maz rebels against her parents' rules by allowing a dark man to read 'a paperback novel called *Distant Lands*' (p.67). The fact that she implicitly gives the man permission to read the book forges a bond between them. She imagines that the man is 'a Pakistani' (p.68) so, like the paperback, he too evokes 'distant lands'.

Key point

The idea of 'distant lands' is alluring because it suggests places so remote that the girl cannot even imagine what they are like. Yet the story suggests that, from the perspective of such an insular township, even the nearest city seems as exotic as a place that is literally 'distant'.

Fat Maz's curiosity about the dark man and the excitement of her 'conspiracy' (p.68) mean that she looks forward to the lunch hours. She even ensures that they will continue by refusing to sell the paperback to 'a big red woman' (p.69). The 'tacit understanding' (p.69) she shares with the man brings unexpected rewards. As she perceives his excitement on approaching the ending of *Distant Lands*, she realises that 'she was happy' (p.70) – a feeling Fat Maz seems almost unfamiliar with.

'For the bus'

When the man finishes reading the novel he thanks Fat Maz and gives her fifty dollars 'for the bus' (p.70). There is no suggestion that Fat Maz is too poor to buy a bus ticket, so the value of the gift lies in the independence it grants her – the ability to bypass her parents, and also the idea, never suggested by her parents, that she *should* leave the town and make her own life in the world. It is this idea, as much as her sudden (albeit limited) financial independence, which brings her to life: she confronts her parents at the door and 'fairly crackled' (p.71) with a new-found energy.

Q How does the narrative suggest that the alternative realities hinted at in the story are preferable to the reality of the here-and-now?

'Laps' (pp.73–87)

Summary: *Queenie Cookson talks her husband, Cleve, and their daughter, Dot, into revisiting Angelus, Queenie's childhood home and the scene of traumatic events in the past.*

Like the Nilsams, the Cooksons are a family of three in which past events haunt the married couple but their young child gives a sense of meaning and direction to their lives. In contrast to most of the stories about the Nilsams, though, 'Laps' focuses on the wife and mother, Queenie, and her attempt to confront and jettison her memories of traumatic incidents.

Queenie's swimming as therapy

After spending seven years rebuilding her life in the city, Queenie swims laps in the ocean 'between the groynes' (p.75; groynes are timber structures that stabilise the sea floor near the beach). The idea of swimming as therapy – first 'like doing penance', then 'a pleasure' (p.75) – introduces the issue of past hurts in vague terms; the narrative refers to 'a grave and a crusade' (p.75) but the details are only gradually revealed.

Queenie's swimming allows her to reflect on her past and, in a way, to recover some of its strengths, such as the feeling 'she had when she was a girl, when her grandfather was alive' (p.75). This establishes the close connection between Queenie and her (deceased) grandfather who taught her to swim. The end of the story also foregrounds this relationship, so that the narrative forms a loop and generates a sense of closure.

Cleve and Dot

The narrative immediately places a distance between Queenie and her husband and daughter, who 'mooned along the beach indulging her' (p.76). This distance is reinforced by Queenie's detachment during their 'Breakfast Banter' (p.78) and Cleve's reluctance to visit Angelus. The strength of the bond between Cleve and Dot mirrors that between Jerra and Sam Nilsam. Although she is a good surfer, Dot is 'lazy like Cleve' and prefers simply to walk beside him on the beach (p.76). They share a resentment of the development on the Scarborough beachfront, and their shared wit and flair for language at breakfast contrast with Queenie's more serious demeanour.

Returning to Angelus

The weekend visit to Angelus forms the second part of the story. Cleve admits that the trip may help to 'exorcise' bad feelings associated with the place and their pasts. Queenie points to a more positive motive:

'to...confirm things' (p.80). That is, Queenie thinks that they will more readily grasp the distance they have 'travelled' in their lives since leaving Angelus – an emotional distance, as well as the five-hour drive – by returning to it.

The reasons why Queenie became 'the local girl who turned coat' (p.81) are gradually explained. By deferring these details until towards the end of the story, the narrative legitimates Queenie's nostalgia for the town through Dot's approval of the picturesque surroundings and the affectionate description of Queenie's old family home as 'solid and lovely' (p.82). This image of a deeply settled and harmonious existence contrasts with the recent lives of the Cooksons and also with the images to which the narrative next turns, of the whaling industry.

The whaling industry

The details of Queenie's participation in protests against the whaling industry are revealed when the family drives to Paris Bay, the site of 'the flensing deck where Queenie had lain in the blood and offal with the others' (p.84). The repeated references to blood, the description of the vast tank for storing whale oil and Queenie's recollection of the 'stench of burning blubber' (p.84) all evoke the grotesque, violent nature of the industry. The narrative's sympathies are in accordance with those of the characters. Although there is a feeling of pathos about the abandoned jetty, there is also a sense that the whaling industry is an aspect of the past that should certainly be left *in* the past.

Finally, Queenie takes Cleve and Dot to what had been her grandfather's farm. The 'KEEP OUT' sign on the gate and the caretaker's refusal to let them in are indicative of the changes that have taken place, and also of the limited extent to which Queenie can actually revisit the past. She is even denied access to her grandfather's grave on the hill, suggesting that the present-day owners of the property are somewhat mean and spiteful. Nevertheless, defying these prohibitions, Queenie drives down to the beach. All the complexities and tensions of Queenie's past are bound together on this beach: it is where Dot was conceived, but also where a pod of whales became stranded (described at the end of Winton's novel *Shallows*, and obliquely alluded to in this story) and where Queenie and Cleve's marriage had foundered.

Although the Cooksons clearly have established a new and more contented life, these past events still weigh heavily on Queenie and she takes to the ocean in order to 'swim it all out' (p.87). Here, the narrative returns to the opening images of swimming and of emotional 'weights'. Queenie's actions indicate the need for a conscious engagement with troubling issues from the past – to be 'not invincible but strong' (p.87).

Q How do interactions between people and their environments in 'Laps' such as whaling, farming, housing and construction) suggest differences between the past and the present? Does the story suggest that things were better or worse in the past, or neither?

'Bay of Angels' (pp.89–93)

Summary: *Jerra and a friend go to a bay to talk and swim; Jerra fondly remembers the place from his childhood, but his friend starts to cry.*

Although the first-person narrator of 'Bay of Angels' is unnamed, the narrative strongly suggests that Jerra Nilsam is the narrator through his reference to his son as 'little Sam' (p.92). Unusually for the Nilsam stories, here Jerra is contented and talkative, appreciating the beauty of the setting and the peaceful interactions between people and the natural environment. Even the city is humanised, with its towers taking the 'white sun on their flanks' (p.91). The yachts seem other-worldly, 'like light and music' (p.91) or with sails 'like the wings of angels' (p.93).

In contrast, Jerra's friend is so distressed that he 'saw nothing' of the scene's beauty (p.91) and, despite Jerra's efforts at conversation, he says nothing. During these afternoons his mother-in-law looks after his wife and children, and he thinks that these times help him 'stay afloat' (p.91). These facts suggest that one family member is very ill, but leave the details unspecified. Jerra thinks of his friend as someone who 'didn't know what it meant to seize up altogether' (p.92). However, this afternoon he tires quickly, and when Jerra prompts him with a direct question – 'Is she worse?' – the friend 'began to weep' (p.93).

In a sense, Jerra's almost ecstatic sense of being 'alive' (p.92) blinds him to his friend's true emotional state. Jerra seems shocked at the emotional distance between them, emphasised by the juxtaposition of the lines 'My heart fattened with joy' and 'My friend began to weep' (p.93). Despite the closeness of their friendship, the two men are, in fact, entirely alone. Just as Jerra perceives that he is 'in the world outside of [his friend]' (p.91), so too is the friend outside Jerra's world.

Q Explain the sentence: 'Hanging strangled in a net, a gull swung above the water like a cheap symbol in a film' (p.93). What would the gull be a symbol of in this story?

Q The title of this story echoes the name of the town in the previous story, Angelus. What is the significance of this similarity?

'The Strong One' (pp.95–104)

Summary: *Rachel decides to study social work at university; Jerra is daunted by the prospect of looking after Sam; they drive back to Jerra's parents, and learn that Jerra's friend Sean has died, and that Jerra's father is ill.*

This is the only story about the Nilsams that is narrated from Rachel's point of view and she emerges here as a complex character in her own right. Set in the summer following 'Forest Winter', the story gains considerable energy from Rachel's renewed sense of purpose. Her thoughts about the past are more focused than Jerra's, which allows the narrative to reveal aspects of the Nilsams' personal histories – 'the band folding, the pregnancy they couldn't decide to end' (p.101) – from a fresh perspective.

'It's time you followed me'

Rachel's decision to study social work signals a change to the family's material circumstances: to where they live, how they generate their income and who will look after Sam. However, the most important change is to Rachel's perception of her own identity. In the opening scene, Rachel sees her reflection in a window and is heartened by the outward appearance of her restored health: her 'belly…looked as firm as it felt' (p.97).

Rachel's refreshed identity alters the balance of power between Rachel and Jerra. Previously, the family's movements had been on Jerra's initiative, and Rachel now reasons with him on the basis of equality: 'I reckon it's time you followed me for a while' (p.99). Jerra is 'scared' at the prospect of becoming Sam's primary caregiver because he 'won't be able to do it properly' (p.100), but Rachel shows her level-headedness when she responds: 'How do you think I felt?' (p.100). This passage effectively demolishes old, conservative arguments for men earning the income and women staying at home with the children. As if to emphasise her new, powerful role in the family hierarchy, Rachel sinks her teeth into Jerra's shoulder.

Rachel's feeling of strength

Jerra and Rachel's relationship is increasingly strained as a result of their differing attitudes towards the past and future. On Christmas morning, rather than going to church Rachel and Jerra take Sam to the beach. The water imagery suggests that they do share moments of peace, watching 'the sea move and sigh and disguise itself in the glitter of sunlight' (p.101). This sentence captures in its rhythms the undulations of the water, suggesting the fluctuations of light and shade, of contentment and despair, in their lives.

Rachel is impatient to make a change 'for the better' (p.101), but Jerra seems more immersed in the past than the present. Jerra begins to reminisce when he recognises a place where he had camped with his friend Sean, and Rachel accuses him of being 'like an old man who can't handle the present' (p.102). As if to convey her eagerness to head into the future she quickly pushes Sam up the hill, leaving Jerra behind. Rachel realises that this is indicative of what their lives will be like; she will lead, and Jerra will follow.

This newly-established order confirms to Rachel that she has an inner strength not previously acknowledged. The meaning of the title becomes explicit: Rachel is 'the strong one' (p.103), and her 'strength' lies not only in her ability to survive, but also in her capacity to refashion her life.

The past intrudes into the present

Rachel drives the family to Jerra's parents' house. The symbolism of Rachel being 'in the driver's seat' is consistent with her now setting the agenda for the family, but she cannot completely control everything that happens to them. As they approach the house, Jerra has a strong feeling that something is wrong. Rachel is determined not to be swayed from her course and she warns Jerra not to 'stuff it up' (p.104). However, when she sees Jerra's mother looking 'swollen-eyed and shaky' (p.104) Rachel also realises that there are problems.

Jerra's intuitive feeling is proven to be accurate when his mother tells him that Sean died on the previous day. Here, Jerra's sensitivity to the past allows him to apprehend something that Rachel was ignorant of, and she experiences 'a chink of panic' (p.104). As if to show that the past is not completely threatening, Jerra's mother takes Rachel's hand, and Rachel feels 'strength there' (p.104).

Q What is the significance of Rachel saying she will cut her hair off (p.102)?

Q Why do you think the story ends with the odd image of Sam baring his teeth at Jerra's mother?

'Holding' (pp.105–16)

Summary: *Hart, a nurse, depends on the friendship of Clive Genders, a wealthy executive; Hart dreams that Clive's wife, Jan, dies from a miscarriage; Jan does have a miscarriage, but survives.*

Like 'Bay of Angels', 'Holding' explores the sustaining powers of friendship and also the way in which friends can become isolated and introverted at times of distress. Hart and Clive are so different from one another that Hart thinks of Clive as a 'friendly alien' (p.107). Clive manages 'several companies', is a member of the Liberal Party, has expensive tastes and is religious (pp.107–8). In contrast, Hart is a non-believer, works as a nurse and, apart from the extravagant meals he shares with Clive, lives simply – choosing to eat at a 'greasy little pinball joint' when Clive cancels their lunch appointment one Friday (p.114).

A more significant difference between the men is that Clive is married and has children, whereas Hart is separated from his wife, Andrea, and is childless. This difference becomes increasingly telling, with Clive seemingly able to cope with his wife's miscarriage while Hart despairs at the lack of meaning in his life. By the end of the story, Clive's friendship is the only thing Hart feels capable of 'holding onto' (p.116).

Lunch at Picnicks

Hart and Clive's lunch at Picnicks restaurant provides a unique view of the city in these stories. In 'Bay of Angels', Jerra sees the city across the water but he does not view it as an insider. Clive and Hart, however, seem at home in this high-class restaurant, where they are on first-name terms with the waiter Nick and calmly look down on the city streets 'watching the traffic pass' (p.111). However, the elegant yet sterile surrounds of the restaurant are at odds with Hart's 'strange feelings of grief and anxiety', which he feels unable to express in this context (p.112).

Hart's work as a nurse

In keeping with his name, Hart works in a field where his 'heart' – his capacity to empathise with people – is involved. The narrative implies that he is a psychiatric nurse, which is ironic because Hart's own psychological state is damaged but none of his knowledge proves useful to him.

Hart despairs at being unable to treat the boy who 'prolapses his anus' (p.111). The boy's behaviour can be read as an attempt to turn himself inside out, to expose his interior self to the world. This is precisely what Hart finds himself unable to do on an emotional level; he cannot express his innermost feelings of emptiness and loss. It is significant, then, that when Hart says, 'I am not coping', he thinks of the boy 'turning his arse out in a corner', and then in a first gesture of sympathy Hart opens up his own fists (p.114).

Sources of meaning

If lunches in a fine restaurant and work as a nurse do not offer Hart any sources of consolation or purpose, the narrative does point to two possible sources of meaning that are lacking from Hart's life. These are a family and a religious belief. The crisis of Jan's miscarriage brings Clive and Jan closer together, whereas Hart's sense of loss seems to deepen each day. His house feels 'big and empty...still hollow without Andrea' (p.113), and Hart experiences this emptiness as a loss within himself, or even *of* himself – that is, of his identity.

Hart watches Bishop Desmond Tutu on television; Tutu is a black South African religious leader who became internationally known during the struggle against apartheid in the 1980s. Hart thinks of Desmond Tutu as 'a man who'd found himself' (p.113), and thus as a man radically different from Hart in his sense of purpose and his obvious value to his countrymen.

Clive is inspired by Tutu, and even phones him to ask 'a few naïve questions' (p.112). As unlikely as this scenario may seem, it suggests that, despite the obvious polarity between the white capitalist and the black bishop, Clive Genders and Bishop Desmond Tutu are both believers and might at least be able to converse about matters of the spirit. Hart, though, is a sceptic. In his dream about being in a funeral procession he imagines leaping from 'an armoured car' – indicative of the way Hart tries to insulate himself from the world – and approaching Bishop Desmond Tutu. The bishop, however, signals to Hart 'to keep away' (p.116), reinforcing Hart's feelings of alienation and bewilderment.

Q Explain the irony of the name of the restaurant at which Clive and Hart have lunch: 'Picnicks'.

'More' (pp.117–31)

Summary: *Jerra has an affair; Rachel prepares for university exams but she and Jerra argue, Jerra cuts his finger and Sam seems to swallow Ratsak; Rachel decides they should stay with Jerra's parents; Jerra's father is terminally ill.*

'More' is set some time after 'The Strong One', but before 'Gravity'. The first part is fragmented in structure, reflecting the way in which Rachel and Jerra's lives lurch from crisis to crisis. The second section partially relieves these tensions, though adds the additional complication of Jerra's father, Tom, being terminally ill with cancer.

I: 'Everything is not all right'

The story opens with Jerra coming home late at night and choosing to sleep in Sam's room. That he pushes his clothes 'deep into the laundry basket' (p.119) is the first sign that he has been with another woman. However, Jerra's affair is not confirmed until several pages later, when he recalls the liaison: '*He saw that she was not Rachel*' (p.123). The narrative's withholding of details reflects both Jerra's inability to talk to Rachel about his feelings and Rachel's refusal to discuss the incident.

'More' exposes how Jerra's actions and his difficulty in dealing with emotional tensions impact on those close to him. Rachel suggests that in playing chess Jerra uses the 'tactics of a blind bull' (p.120), and this blunt disregard for the wellbeing of others characterises Jerra's behaviour generally. The reference to Hemingway, who often wrote about Spanish bullfights, is significant because Hemingway's style, like Winton's throughout much of *Minimum of Two*, features minimal description and short, terse lines of dialogue in which the characters attempt to reveal as little as possible of their interior selves.

Jerra cuts his finger badly while chopping lemons, and this self-inflicted wound is reminiscent of the boy cutting himself in 'No Memory Comes'. It suggests that Jerra's attitude towards life is bitter and self-destructive, even though he may think he is acting for his own pleasure.

II: 'Don't be bitter, be better'

In the second part of the story the focus shifts away from Jerra and Rachel's relationship towards Jerra's relationship with his father. The shared meal of rivercrabs, with its 'florid mess' and 'eating noise and baby talk' (p.127) suggesting the messy communality of family life, forces Jerra to think of himself as part of a larger whole. He walks out seemingly in self-disgust, but later he plays the guitar (hampered by his bandaged finger) for his father and they have their only conversation in these stories.

Jerra's father is always referred to as 'his father' or 'the old man', rather than by his name, Tom; this emphasises his relationship to Jerra over his independent identity. In this scene he takes on the role almost of a religious 'father', such as a priest, who does not need to press Jerra for details in order to give pertinent advice. Moreover, knowing 'how long he's got left' (p.129) has forced him to reflect on life in a way few of Winton's characters – in any of these stories – think is necessary or desirable.

Key point

Jerra's father tells Jerra not to dwell on his 'losses', but rather to follow his mother's advice: 'don't be bitter, be better' (p.129). This is, in fact, a message that is central to *Minimum of Two* as a whole: not to be overwhelmed by loss, but to rise above it.

At this point the meaning of the story's title becomes apparent. Jerra's father says 'there's more to it' (p.129) – that is, there is more to life than its surface appearances. Jerra is surprised to find *The Book of Common Prayer* by his father's chair, suggesting that Jerra's father had not previously been religious but is now drawn to discover what 'more' there is to life.

Quail

Rachel and Jerra are partially reconciled at the end of the story. They walk together through the bush, eventually touching and on the verge of kissing. They are startled, however, by the sudden flight of quail from the undergrowth. Winton's choice of the type of bird is quite deliberate, since it allows Rachel to say 'Quail' (p.131), not just identifying the birds but as if giving an instruction to Jerra. Whereas previously Rachel had described Jerra as like 'a blind bull' (p.120), now she is (albeit inadvertently) telling him to cower, to show some fear and thereby acknowledge the fragility and impermanence of his own being in the world.

Q What is the meaning of the unusual expression: 'he heard the blood beating at his throat' (p.120)?

'Death Belongs to the Dead, His Father Told Him, And Sadness to the Sad' (pp.133–8)

Summary: *The Man turns a blind eye to the misfortunes of others, but he is drawn to the Dying Gentleman; when the Gentleman dies, The Man holds him in his arms.*

The abstract, philosophical qualities of 'Death Belongs to the Dead...' give it some of the attributes of a parable or Morality Play. In these narrative forms, the psychology of individual characters is less important than the abstract entities for which they stand and the overall 'message' of the story (see Themes & Issues: Moments of Revelation and Acceptance). The setting of 'Death Belongs to the Dead...' is established only in general terms such as 'the street and the café' and 'the old pub on the corner' (p.135), and the two central characters are named only as 'The Man' and 'the Dying Gentleman'.

One abstract entity that is personified in the story is death. The Man thinks of the junkies as 'the dead' (p.135), partly because they appear to have no meaningful activities (such as work) in their lives and partly because their drug addiction places them at serious risk of dying. The Man also thinks of the voice of the Dying Gentleman as 'the voice of death' (p.136). It is because he thinks of death as an entity separate from himself that, at least initially, he feels no compassion for these individuals.

The moral of the story

The Man's attitude towards those who are (at least in his eyes) close to death is informed by his father's advice: 'Death belongs to the dead, his father told him, and sadness to the sad' (p.135 and the story's title). Although The Man lives as if he can keep sadness and death at a comfortable distance, the narrative describes his gradual recognition that this is not a sustainable life philosophy.

Increasingly, The Man is drawn to the Dying Gentleman, who retains his dignity despite his physical decline. Indeed, the Gentleman gains a kind of spiritual purity, signified by the sunlight forming a 'tonsure', a 'monkish spot' (p.136) on his head. (A tonsure is the shaved crown of the head of a priest or monk.) The Man comments to the Gentleman that it is a 'Sad world' (p.137), acknowledging for the first time that sadness is part of everyone's life and thus implicitly questioning his father's advice.

As the Gentleman exhales for the last time, The Man holds him and sees 'the black hole of his mouth…it seemed to go forever down' (p.138). There is no suggestion of an afterlife or of a soul escaping the confines of the body; rather, there seems only to be an empty chasm. The Man now realises that death does not belong only to 'the dead' but is a universal condition, perhaps only 'a breath away' (p.138). In the absence of moral or religious certainties, the story suggests that a world in which the living show compassion for the dying is preferable to one in which each man fends for himself and does 'not look over his shoulder' (p.135).

Q What is the significance of the second section of the story, in which the Man sees 'a thin, dark man holding a cleaver' (p.137) but walks straight past?

'Blood and Water' (pp.139–53)

Summary: *Rachel goes into labour but experiences problems; the midwife, Annie, decides Rachel should go to hospital; the baby is in the breech position; the labour lasts eighteen hours, the birth is traumatic but Rachel and the baby cling to life; they call him Sam.*

The story of Sam Nilsam's birth is the earliest set of the Nilsam stories. Opening with an optimistic tone at the onset of Rachel's labour, the narrative initially represents Jerra and Rachel's determination to shun hospitals and doctors in a positive manner, but gradually introduces complexities. The presence of a midwife whom they have 'come to love', the fires burning 'in the stove and the fireplace', Rachel's laughter and Jerra's assertion that it will be the 'happiest night of my life' (p.141) all suggest that the baby will be born into abundant warmth and love. Against these emotions, the ensuing tensions and the clinical way in which medical staff take control of the birth appear all the more starkly.

The significance of blood and water

The epigraph to 'Blood and Water' is a quotation from the Gospel of St John, and it both (partly) explains the significance of the title and introduces the issue of religious belief. The quotation describes the flow of blood and water from Christ's body when it is pierced by a soldier's spear. So, it is significant that the story begins with water – the amniotic fluid that has cushioned the baby in the womb – running down Rachel's leg.

This link between biblical allusion and the onset of labour suggests that pregnancy and childbirth are akin to spiritual experiences, although Jerra and Rachel may not think in these terms when the labour begins. Indeed, they regard Annie's religious belief as slightly eccentric; only later does Jerra acknowledge that there may be a religious dimension to his experiences in the delivery room.

The religious associations of the epigraph resonate with the prayer that Jerra remembers his mother singing to him when he was a child. What is at first an innocent-sounding verse that Jerra imagines singing to his own child 'out of nostalgia' (p.142) becomes charged with meaning, and Jerra's hope that a divine being might 'look upon a little child' (p.142) with pity comes very close to a genuine religious belief.

The midwife and the hospital staff

The hopefulness of the story's opening is largely attributable to the presence of the midwife, Annie. She is 'gentle' (p.141), her tone is light and informal, and she asks Rachel 'How do you feel?' (p.143) before she makes a decision. However, once they go to hospital Annie and Rachel relinquish control of the birth to the nurses and doctors.

In contrast to Annie, the hospital staff treat Rachel as merely a component part in a medical procedure, divesting her of dignity and agency. At first they are disdainful of the Nilsams' endeavour to have a home birth, then they are sarcastic about Jerra's request for an ultrasound: 'All that technology' somebody quips (p.144).

Key point

The narrative does not individualise the hospital staff, but refers to them as 'nurses and orderlies' (p.143), 'a masked face' (p.144) or 'the smock' (p.145). This has the effect of representing the staff in terms of their function within the hospital system, emphasising the tendency of the system to reduce the people within it – medical staff as well as patients – to the status of objects.

The baby is born when the gynaecologist, Doctor O'Donelly, intervenes after Rachel's eighteen-hour labour. Annie refers to the doctor as 'The Knife' (p.146), anticipating the violence with which he delivers the baby. He uses scissors to cut Rachel, and the baby is pulled out with hands and forceps; the story's title is invoked in the 'rush of blood and water' at the moment of birth (p.149). Winton uses short sentences with a minimum of adjectives to emphasise the shocking nature of the action, making this a frank, unapologetic account of a traumatic birth.

Jerra stays with Rachel throughout the labour and communicates calmly and clearly with the staff despite their antipathy towards him. The level of detail in their observations suggests that Jerra and Rachel have spent many hours in careful preparation for the birth. Jerra identifies merconium when the baby first becomes visible, and Rachel insists she does not want 'syndemitrine', anticipating the doctor's thoughts exactly (p.148).

The hospital staff casually dismiss Jerra and Rachel's knowledge and wishes, and they talk in clipped sentences that lack a subject. For instance, 'Too late for a C-section' (p.146) and 'No heartbeat' (p.149) do not indicate the *person* who might have had a C-section or is lacking a heartbeat. Nevertheless, the narrative provides some justification for their attitudes. The lack of an earlier ultrasound means that the breech presentation is not diagnosed until too late, eliminating the possibility of a Caesarean operation. As a result, the birth is horrific and seriously threatens the health of both Rachel and the baby. Moreover, the staff handle the baby with extreme care and expertise; their 'hands were gentle' and 'there was grace in the plying of his limbs' (p.150).

'Call him Samuel'

Throughout the birth, the clinical approach of the hospital staff is contrasted with Jerra's sense of the experience as a spiritual one. In his mind Jerra pleads with a Christ whose existence he hitherto had been sceptical of. When the baby's chest fills with air, it is as if a divine presence has entered the room, transforming a medical procedure into a life-giving event.

Annie's suggestion to name the baby Samuel is an allusion to the Old Testament story of Hannah, who prayed to God for a son. When Hannah finally gave birth she called her son Samuel, which sounds like the Hebrew for 'heard of God'.[3] Annie also thinks of Sam as a kind of gift from God.

Jerra, though, sees Sam as a product of more worldly processes. When the paediatrician says that Sam is 'strong' Jerra suggests he is 'Like his mother' in this (p.151, recalling 'The Strong One'). And at night when Jerra sneaks into the intensive care unit to see his son, he 'gripped an arm... felt blood' (p.153). This 'blood' means both that Sam is alive and that he belongs to Rachel and Jerra in the most fundamental sense: 'This one's mine', Jerra affirms, in the last words of the book.

[3] 1 Samuel 20, *The Holy Bible: New International Version*, Hodder and Stoughton, London, 1988.

CHARACTERS & RELATIONSHIPS

Jerra Nilsam

Key quotes

'He was thankful for Rachel and the baby. They were something to check himself against' (p.6, 'Forest Winter').

'Nilsam wrote songs and sold them to singers who never quite sang them well enough or in the presence of people influential enough to make him rich. They were not love songs and not particularly sad' (p.30, 'Gravity').

'Jerra seemed to bear weights from the past as though they were treasures he had to take with him' (p.98, 'The Strong One').

As the central character in six of the fourteen stories, Jerra Nilsam is the dominant figure in *Minimum of Two*. He is not without his faults, but on the whole his values are endorsed by the narratives: he is committed to his family; he enjoys simple things in life and has few material wants; he dislikes hypocrisy but appreciates warmth and honesty. On the other hand, Jerra can be very nostalgic about the past and he is poor at communicating his feelings. Both of these negative traits cause problems in his marriage, and there are moments when Rachel fiercely resents him; in 'The Strong One' she accuses him of being 'like an old man who can't handle the present' (p.102). The stories validate Rachel's accusation to a certain extent, although they also show how hard Jerra's (and Rachel's) circumstances are. As Rachel acknowledges, the winter of Sam's birth is particularly difficult because of their limited finances and Rachel's long recuperation, and Jerra becomes 'stiff and hard with surviving' (p.101).

A more positive aspect of Jerra's fondness for the past is presented in 'Bay of Angels'. He remembers his mother bringing him to the beach that he visits with a friend, a beach where he 'learnt to walk on that soft strip of sand' (p.91). This gestures to a continuity of habitation and a sense of belonging to place that elsewhere in these stories is seriously threatened by modern development and mobility. Jerra remembers people gathering together here, 'laughing and wading with nets and calling after children' (p.92). This mode of reminiscence idealises the past, but Jerra's memories help generate such pleasure that he forgets he is swimming; he is literally 'buoyed up' by his memories. This is a rare instance in *Minimum of Two* of memories not acting like a 'weight', but in fact having the opposite effect.

Jerra finds contentment as a father

If there are times when Jerra struggles to 'handle the present', such as the time when he has an affair (referred to in 'More') or on the anniversary of his father's death in 'Gravity', then there are other times of real crisis when Jerra shows commitment and resilience. In 'Forest Winter' Rachel has a near-fatal asthma attack, but Jerra's determination to obtain Ventolin for her – overcoming the pharmacist's reluctance to dispense the medicine – enables him to save her life. In 'Blood and Water' Jerra remains steadfastly by Rachel's side throughout her difficult labour. At home he had 'rubbed oil on her lips...massaged the small of her back' (p.142), and then in the hospital he breathes alongside her and communicates as well as possible with the hospital staff.

Sam's traumatic birth marks a turning point in both Jerra and Rachel's lives. In 'Forest Winter', set nine weeks later than 'Blood and Water', Jerra reflects on the previous few months and is 'almost catatonic from misery' (p.3). He takes a long time to accept his changed circumstances: the failure of his work as a musician, Rachel's decision to study, and his new role as Sam's primary carer. The illness and death of Jerra's father marks another transition, a period during which Jerra increasingly values his family and his role within it. In 'Nilsam's Friend', by which time Sam is a toddler, Jerra's acceptance of having 'a son to look after, and a wife to consider' (p.44) allows him to feel more contented than at any other point in these stories.

Although Jerra can be introverted and uncommunicative, he also has a strong creative aspect. This is manifest in his work as a musician, which includes not only playing but composing too. Perhaps Jerra's most significant characteristic of all is his skill and enjoyment in being a father to Sam. The difficulties of Sam's first weeks of life are clear in 'Forest Winter' and from Jerra's recollection of a night when he 'tore Sam from his neck and...shook him till his head might come away' (p.121, 'More'). However, the bond between Jerra and Sam only grows stronger with time, and is especially evident in their conversations in 'Gravity'; Rachel and Sam are never represented talking to each other in this way. Jerra's friend also affirms Jerra's skill as a father, saying 'You're good with him' as Jerra gives Sam a kiss (p.45). In this way, Jerra represents a male character who is able and willing to take on roles within the family that men of his father's generation would have been far less comfortable with.

Men and masculinity

Key quotes

'Nilsam shrugged. He felt dowdy. He was a man and he felt dowdy the way women were supposed to feel dowdy' (p.45, 'Nilsam's Friend').

'I just liked wood, happy to work as my own boss...' (p.56, 'Minimum of Two').

In some ways, Winton's male characters conform to a conventional Australian male 'type'. They drink beer, like to work with their hands, are not highly educated yet are independent and highly protective of their families. They are reticent about expressing their feelings, even to the point of being inarticulate. For instance, Madigan's inability to communicate exacerbates the difficulties in his marriage; he 'wanted so much to talk' but he 'said nothing' (p.60, 'Minimum of Two'). Similarly, in 'Gravity' Jerra 'couldn't bring himself to mention his father' (p.28) despite the tension caused by his refusal to articulate his feelings.

In other ways, these men have unexpected attributes and perform roles quite different from those of the stereotype. Within the family they frequently undertake duties traditionally associated with women. Cleve Cookson cooks the breakfast (p.78, 'Laps'), and Jerra looks after Sam (in 'Gravity' and 'Nilsam's Friend'). Madigan's workshop is a stereotypical male domain, but Jerra's music studio reflects a creative, bohemian aspect to male identity. Also at odds with the stereotype is the fact that none of these male characters plays sport or meets his mates in the pub. Indeed, for Hart the pub is where he realises how much he has lost. It is the place where Hart and his wife, Andrea, became engaged, then argued 'the terms of separation', and finally where he sits alone, drinking 'in tempo with that horrible slipping feeling' (p.115, 'Holding').

Although the male characters work, they do not have positions with much power or prestige. Hart is a nurse – probably a psychiatric nurse – and Cleve in 'Laps' also works in a hospital. They are not doctors, and indeed Hart is disdainful of what he views as the psychiatrists' 'useless academic curiosity' (p.113). For Hart, the question is not about power but about how worthwhile his work is, and Hart resents being subjected to the artificial constraints imposed by the time frame for treating a patient by the 'case conference at the end of the week' (p.113).

Jerra saws wood in 'Forest Winter' but music is his real profession and his passion. On its own, though, music does not provide the level of financial security his family requires. Instead, Jerra learns to find sources of fulfilment and meaning through being a father to Sam and a husband to Rachel. These familial roles are also fulfilling for other fathers in the stories, such as Clive in 'Holding' and Cleve in 'Laps'.

Clive Genders certainly enjoys the affluent lifestyle that comes with managing 'several companies' (p.107). However, 'Holding' makes it clear that Clive's sense of purpose in life devolves much more from his family and religious faith than from material success. In contrast, male characters who are single and childless, such as Hart, or Jerra's friend who travels overseas, lack such purpose or secure sense of identity.

Rachel Nilsam

Key quotes

'In her ocean of new feeling she knew she had to be the strong one' (p.103, 'The Strong One').

'She'd had to jettison more than he had to stay afloat: the lousy luggage of family memory, the self-hatred other men had seized upon and cultivated – even bearing Sam and having him torn out by force' (p.98, 'The Strong One').

Rachel Nilsam is an assertive, resilient character who plays a supportive yet crucial role in the stories about her and Jerra. She has survived a troubled personal history to discover within herself a strength of will and resourcefulness that seem to exceed Jerra's. Her calm, practical response to Jerra's temporary blindness in 'Forest Winter' – 'Don't be wet', she chides him when he avoids telling her if he can see (p.9) – establishes these qualities very effectively. However, since the narrative point of view is mostly aligned with Jerra's perspective, Rachel remains a relatively enigmatic figure, not least because Jerra himself often finds her difficult to understand. One positive aspect to this narrative perspective is that Rachel's physical appearance is described whereas Jerra's isn't: Rachel is 'tall and slim.... Her tan made her look as though she was made from polished jarrah' (p.27, 'Gravity').

Only in 'The Strong One' does the reader perceive Rachel's situation from her own perspective. She reflects on her past difficulties that never seem to be in Jerra's thoughts: 'the lousy luggage of family memory, the self-hatred other men had seized upon and cultivated' (p.98). She also views Jerra from a critical perspective in 'The Strong One' that contrasts strongly with his own tendency towards self-pity and melancholy (in 'Forest Winter' and 'Gravity', for instance).

Understandably, Rachel finds it frustrating that Jerra keeps 'the deepest...most important things to himself' (p.102), yet Rachel is not represented as a particularly effective communicator herself. She often responds to emotional tensions by crying, as in 'Gravity' when Jerra is late home for the party and in 'More' when they argue. Of course, there are underlying reasons for Rachel's unhappiness, such as Jerra's affair, which she refuses to discuss. She refers obliquely to the affair, declaring that 'I know about it, Jerra' (p.123) and 'lots of things happen that should never happen' (p.124). However, Rachel does not make specific accusations, and later she makes explicit her refusal to talk about Jerra's infidelity: 'I can't listen to you tell me how sorry you are or aren't' (p.125). In this way, Rachel forecloses the possibility of effective communication just as effectively as Jerra often does.

Overall, though, Rachel is much less inclined than Jerra to dwell on their difficulties, and while Jerra's gaze frequently is on the past it is Rachel who looks to the future. Rachel is also more focused on her goals in life than Jerra is. She reflects on 'ten years' of living in caravan parks as a child and wants 'to go', to move on (p.99, 'The Strong One'); Jerra, though, is content for the past to repeat itself over and over. Rachel's decision in 'The Strong One' to gain a professional qualification in social work owes as much to her self-esteem and her confidence to pursue her ambitions as it does to the family's need to have a better standard of living.

Relationships: the significance of the title 'Minimum of Two'

Key quotes

'We chatted and gossiped. We did things. People liked the sight of us together' (p.57, 'Minimum of Two').

'She liked him so much more since Dot was born and they lived here' (p.78, 'Laps').

Minimum of Two shares its title with one of its stories. In 'Minimum of Two', the literal meaning of the phrase is the minimum length of a prison sentence: the number of *years* before parole may be granted (p.50).

However, the resonance of this phrase with the other stories, and hence its appropriateness as the title of the collection, relates to Winton's interest in relationships. Moreover, the cover of the current Penguin edition shows two young boys together, reinforcing the sense that the book's title refers to situations involving a minimum of two *people*. These 'couples' may be friends as in 'No Memory Comes' or 'Nilsam's Friend', or husband and wife as in the stories about Rachel and Jerra, in 'Laps' and in 'Minimum of Two' itself. There are also the transient yet life-altering encounters between strangers in 'Distant Lands' and 'Death Belongs to the Dead...'.

Often the narrative interest lies in what happens to a relationship when a third person becomes involved, such as the addition of Sam to Jerra and Rachel's lives, or in 'Minimum of Two' the intrusion of the rapist, Blakey, into Greta and Madigan's lives. In these cases, the phrase 'minimum of two' suggests that the relationship between two people is only ever a starting point for a family; other people can always place pressure on a relationship, disrupting its dynamics and equanimity. On the other hand, when a child is added the lives of the parents may be immeasurably enhanced. This is suggested by Jerra's surname: he could be considered as being 'Nil' without 'Sam'. In 'Laps', Dot seems to bind her parents together; they talk to each other *through* Dot, and Queenie thinks that she has liked Cleve 'so much more since Dot was born' (p.78).

Relationships between men and women

Key quotes

> 'Jerra was stiff and hard with surviving; sometimes she didn't know him at all' (p.101, 'The Strong One').
>
> 'Her body would be shut tight; she'd be lying there hard and straight in our bed where things used to be whole and sweet' (p.62, 'Minimum of Two').

Minimum of Two represents male-female relationships as potentially rewarding yet invariably troubled. Several stories explore the ongoing effects of marital breakdowns on individuals. In 'Holding' the focus is on the husband, whereas in 'No Memory Comes' and 'The Water Was Dark...' the central characters are children who have lost their fathers.

The struggle of single-parent families to survive financially is certainly acknowledged, but Winton gives more prominence to the emotional problems that are often experienced by such families. For instance, while 'The Water Was Dark...' suggests that the mother and daughter have a minimal standard of material comfort – their home is a sixth-floor flat in the city – it also represents the lack of warmth and affection between them as being much more destructive. In 'No Memory Comes', the boy refuses to acknowledge the reality of change after his father leaves. This event means the boy's mother must work but, more importantly, it leads to the boy becoming engrossed in the past, insisting to himself that 'things are the same' (p.17) when they evidently are not.

In other stories, even though marriages survive they are haunted by past difficulties and tested by persistent tensions in the present. Cleve and Queenie in 'Laps' have had one breakdown of their marriage in the past, and there remains an emotional distance between them largely due to Queenie's preoccupation with past events. Their daughter, Dot, is a kind of conduit between them, but Queenie's desire to revisit Angelus is not shared by Cleve.

Although Winton's married couples desire intimacy and affection, they struggle to give or receive them. Rachel and Jerra's mutual commitment is evident in 'Forest Winter' when each acts unhesitatingly to assist the other, yet they exchange few kind or gentle words. Rachel feels that Jerra keeps 'the deepest, the most important things to himself' (p.102, 'The Strong One'), while Jerra is perplexed by the changes in Rachel's demeanour following Sam's birth and then when she is determined to study social work. In 'Distant Lands', the girl's parents spend their days in silence and are never represented talking to each other, or indeed experiencing any form of pleasure. Hart recalls his marriage to Andrea in terms of its 'clutching unhappiness' (p.109, 'Holding'), reflecting his sense that he was almost as alone in an emotional sense during his marriage as he is after it has ended.

In 'Minimum of Two', Greta and Madigan are incapable of articulating their feelings to each other, and emotional closeness between them is an increasingly distant memory. Madigan's attempt to reassure Greta by telling her that 'Blakey will pay' (p.57) only places a greater distance between them. Madigan is so desperate to reclaim the intimacy and affection of his marriage that he commits murder – which, of course, only makes the restoration of his marriage even less likely.

Fathers and sons

Key quotes

'He was dead. Actually, finally dead. And now there was nothing for Jerra Nilsam to fall against' (p.29, 'Gravity').

'[The boy's mother] tells him his father is not coming back from Hong Kong because he has fallen in love with the housegirl' (p.15, 'No Memory Comes').

Relationships between fathers and sons are central in these stories, including those such as 'No Memory Comes' in which the father is mostly absent. The loss of one's father is a very traumatic experience for these male characters; for Jerra it is only on the anniversary of his father's death that he begins fully to accept its reality. An interesting contrast is the girl in 'The Water Was Dark...', who shows no real sense of loss even though her father left when she was five years old. Rather, the girl's difficulties are tied to her relationship with her mother, whom the girl hopes to leave 'as soon as she was old enough' (p.39).

Winton represents fathers as casting long shadows over the lives of their sons. In 'Death Belongs To The Dead...', The Man follows his father's instruction to 'not look over his shoulder' (p.135) – in other words, to maintain an emotional detachment from those who are dying or distressed. However, his contact with the Dying Gentleman makes him realise his father was not correct because it is a 'Sad world' (p.137) and death is perhaps only 'a breath away' (p.138). In 'No Memory Comes', the boy responds to the loss of his father by clinging to the past, telling a story 'about how he once caught so many prawns in the river with his father' (p.18) while his friend and his friend's girlfriend make love in the front seat of the car. The boy's friend has moved confidently into adolescence, but the boy still lives imaginatively in his childhood, in a world where his father is forever present.

Jerra Nilsam's relationship with his father is not an easy one, but although there are several references to past tensions between Jerra and his father they are not described in any detail. The reader gains most information about this relationship from Rachel, who surmises to Jerra that 'You must have jumped down his throat when you were younger' (p.131, 'More'). In 'Gravity', the absence of his father over the course of a year makes Jerra increasingly value, and miss, his father's presence. The studio built by Jerra's father survives as a sign that the bond between father and son transcends differences. Additionally, the stories show Jerra developing a new father-son relationship with his own son, Sam, a relationship that is full of hope for the future.

Although the stories mostly explore the significance of father-son relationships, one story that suggests daughters can also be strongly influenced by father figures is 'Laps'. Queenie's grandfather performed a central role in her life, that of the family member who 'was all she had' (p.76). Just as Jerra's father taught him to ride a bike and had been someone to 'fall against' (p.29), Queenie's grandfather taught her to swim, and it is to swimming that she turns when the weight of the past becomes too pressing. Clearly, then, the stories do not discount the possibility of strong (grand)father-daughter relationships. However, the collection as a whole displays a strong interest in the bond between fathers and sons, and in the sons' inheritance of memories and attitudes, both positive and negative, from their fathers.

Children and adolescents

Key quotes

'Summers go by, but the boy knows everything stays the same. Even at twelve he doesn't feel any older' (p.14, 'No Memory Comes').

'Her body was strong and hard. She was young' (p.38, 'The Water Was Dark...').

Winton represents childhood and adolescence as special times of innocence and sensitivity; on the negative side, though, young people are especially vulnerable to trauma as a result of emotional dislocation. The sudden shocks of change, and in particular the loss of relationships that had seemed to be eternal, leave lasting scars and cause personalities to become set in negative, self-destructive ways. The boy in 'No Memory Comes' looks back on his childhood as a time when there were 'No beginnings...and no endings' (p.18). In contrast, the boy's sudden loss of his father causes an abrupt dislocation to his childhood to which he struggles to adjust over several years.

In 'The Water Was Dark...', the girl responds to a similar discontinuity in her childhood; she was five when her father left, and six when her mother was badly burnt. She hardens herself against the world and effectively denies her own emotional needs and impulses. She exposes herself physically to the world by taking off 'her watch and her bikini' (p.38), but her determination to 'be an engine' (p.36) reflects her denial of feeling, her desire to insulate herself from the world on an emotional level. Her personality, then, is shaped to a large extent by these twin traumas of her childhood: her father's departure, and her mother's decline into chronic depression and alcoholism.

The vulnerability of children to traumatic events is represented through other encounters too. In the second section of 'No Memory Comes', one man commits suicide – appearing to be hopelessly vulnerable – while another, the father of the boy's friend, cruelly punishes his son for wetting the bed. What links the actions of these men is the destructive impact they have on the two boys. These negative images of adult masculinity make the central character even more determined that 'he and his friend will never change' (p.14). However, his desire for things not to change becomes a refusal to recognise or adapt to change, and, as the story makes clear, change is in fact the one constant in his life.

Fat Maz is the oldest of the adolescents in *Minimum of Two*, and she shares with the boy in 'No Memory Comes' a reluctance to enter adulthood and confront the future. However, for Fat Maz this is not because the people and the environment around her continually change, but rather because of the dreary sameness in which people in her town go through the motions of meaningless lives. It is the tantalising promise of otherness, embodied by the 'dark man' and the book *Distant Lands*, that gives her new energy and leads her finally to look 'towards the door' (p.71). The alternative is represented by the 'big red woman' whose life is compromised by 'whatever it was that seemed so patently missing' (p.69). Fat Maz realises that the red woman 'could be me' (p.69) – that is, could be what Fat Maz will become if her life continues in its state of inertia.

The very youngest children in *Minimum of Two* are virtually untouched by life's struggles and traumas, and because of this they offer a valuable perspective on the issues that seem to their parents to be so overwhelming. As Jerra and Sam cycle home in 'Gravity', Sam cries 'Green for go' as the lights change (p.26) when Jerra is very reluctant to 'go'; it is as if Sam (inadvertently) is signalling to Jerra that he can't stop life or avoid present and future responsibilities. In 'Laps', Queenie acknowledges that Dot is 'good counsel' (p.82), and Dot's perception of Angelus, unencumbered by memory, helps Queenie to see the town 'better than she ever had' (p.80). Of course, Dot's innocent way of seeing the world is a simplistic one that cannot take into account the complexities of adult experiences and emotions. Nevertheless, both Sam and Dot offer hope for the future through being free of 'weights from the past' (p.98), and their clear-eyed apprehension of things reminds their parents of a less emotionally burdened mode of being alive.

THEMES & ISSUES

Experiences of loss

Key quotes

'There was a hole in him. Something was lost' (p.29, 'Gravity').

'I knew that I had lost my life' (p.63, 'Minimum of Two').

'After all this time [the house] was still hollow without Andrea, and now he wondered whether he mightn't have lost himself as well' (p.113, 'Holding').

'The stuff found a big emptiness in him' (p.57, 'Forest Winter').

'The boy feels a hole open in him' (p.17, 'No Memory Comes').

Winton's exploration of the destructive effects of loss on people's lives is a complex one, showing not only the seriousness of its impact on personality but also that its long-lasting effects may barely be grasped at the time the loss occurs. Different kinds of loss are recognised; the loss of life, or of a loved one due to death, are at one end of the spectrum, then there are losses that accompany marriage breakdowns, and then the loss of childhood innocence in 'No Memory Comes' is at the other end, less traumatic but with its own challenges and deeply felt responses.

In 'The Water Was Dark...', the loss of the father/husband affects the girl and her mother quite differently; the girl becomes incapable of feeling whereas her mother becomes too preoccupied with emotions. The women experience two polarised psychological responses to grief, but in each case their response is part of what limits their capacity to find happiness.

Key point

Compounding the problems faced by these characters are their own reactions, which include denial, anger, an inability or refusal to communicate their feelings, and a desire to cling to the past through memory and nostalgia. Indeed, the stories suggest that the stubborn refusal of characters to confront and thus move on from their experiences can be the most destructive aspect of loss.

Internalising loss

Winton represents the extremely debilitating effects of loss by describing it in terms of a missing body part. For instance, on the anniversary of his father's death Jerra feels as he imagines an amputee does, 'full of ghostly sensations' (p.25, 'Gravity') and as if there is 'a hole in him' (p.29). This metaphor recurs throughout the collection, reflecting both the profound impact of loss on the psyche and the tendency of characters to internalise loss. This may be an instinctive reaction, but it is not necessarily a helpful one.

The characters suffer even more when they become isolated from those around them and are unable to communicate effectively. The boy in 'No Memory Comes' and Hart in 'Holding' both find themselves in this predicament. Although the boy is devastated by the loss of his father he never speaks of it, and he 'swears things are the same' when in fact almost everything in his life has changed. On graduating from school he 'feels a hole open in him' (p.17), but he is unable to identify either what is missing, or a means of becoming 'whole' again. Instead, like the girl in 'The Water Was Dark...', he attempts to reach a state in which he cannot feel anything, in his case by becoming drunk.

For Hart, the end of his two-year marriage to Andrea, even though it was characterised by a 'clutching unhappiness' (p.109), has an ongoing effect on his emotional health. In fact, it seems as though the more time passes, the more Hart feels the loss of something not simply added to his life, but fundamental to his sense of self: 'he wondered whether he mightn't have lost himself as well' (p.113). Here, internalising loss not only renders Hart incapable of speaking about it, but also leads to a loss of identity. Only Clive offers Hart a sense of stability and a promise that things are 'just a little complicated. Not futile' (p.116) – a philosophy that is supported by the collection of stories as a whole.

The past and the persistence of memory

Key quotes

'The boy bores people at parties. He tells them everything he remembers. He remembers everything' (p.16, 'No Memory Comes').

'The big hands so hairy with pollard. Only a memory now' (p.29, 'Gravity').

'Queenie saw the tiny whalers' cabins, the fallen jetty, some paint-smeared sheds, and she was full of memories' (p.83, 'Laps').

'The past is the past' (p.54, 'Minimum of Two').

The characters in *Minimum of Two* are haunted by their pasts because of the persistence of memory. These pasts include family break-ups, conflicts, a traumatic birth, a rape. As devastating as these events are, the characters are afflicted by a condition that in some ways is just as debilitating: an inability to outlive those pasts, to move on into the present and future. Their memories are, then, like a burden or a curse to them.

The weights of memories

Rachel Nilsam perceives that Jerra 'seemed to bear weights from the past as though they were treasures he had to take with him' (p.98). The idea of the past or memories being like a weight that ought to be shed is also present in 'Laps', when Queenie suggests returning to Angelus and thinks 'there's a weight to lose' (p.77). Thus, when Queenie swims she feels that 'she was shifting more than her own weight' (p.75), although the story suggests that some kind of confrontation with the past – for instance, with the places where traumatic events occurred – is needed before such emotional weights can be significantly eased.

Some memories may indeed be 'treasured' ones, but excessive attachment to them manifests as a crippling fear of the present and future. Jerra feels 'afraid' on the anniversary of his father's death (p.25, 'Gravity'), and on returning home his 'heart contracted' (p.26), reflecting his emotionally burdened state at this time. Rachel perceives that Jerra is 'happy still to mark time' in 'The Strong One' (p.101), and she relates Jerra's refusal to look toward the future to his tendency to let the past gain 'hold of him' (p.102). In 'Laps', Queenie also is 'afraid' at the prospect of returning to Angelus and confronting her past (p.79), yet she perceives that while Dot and Cleve have 'been growing' she has 'gone to fat' (p.75) – a physical state that functions here as a metaphor for psychological inertia.

In 'No Memory Comes', the boy's insistence on keeping aspects of the past alive, by wearing Hawaiian shirts or growing his hair long, are symptomatic of his refusal to recognise the reality of changed circumstances. He comes to have an identificatory dependence on memory and remembering; he knows himself, and others know him, as a person who 'remembers everything' (p.16). Ultimately, though, this dependence on memory and remembering is represented as a *dis*membering force, as the boy's accidental mutilation of his groin at the end of the story indicates.

Leaving the past in the past

Madigan tries to tell himself that the 'past is the past' but he is unable to accept key facts about the past: that 'the rape is over' and 'the man is in gaol' (p.54, 'Minimum of Two'). This story suggests that an event as traumatic as a rape does not simply fade into the past, but causes ongoing difficulties and distress for the victim and those close to her. Although Madigan has no actual memory of the rape, the details he has obtained from Greta and through the trial manifest themselves as persistent images in his mind: 'I saw that heaving white back on Greta...her breasts strangling in his fists' (p.62).

These images place Madigan in a kind of permanent nightmare; they are not memories as such, but they represent a form of the past that seems more real to him than the present. Madigan becomes true to his own name, 'mad', and in the grip of his psychotic state he sets out to commit a murder from which no good can possibly come.

Queenie Cookson represents a more positive engagement with the weight of memories. For Queenie, such a weight *can* be alleviated, but only by persistent effort and only by accepting the realities of both the past and the present.

Memories as vital connections

If the stories suggest that people struggle when memories become more real to them than their present situations, they also acknowledge that memory provides a vital connection to the past, allowing for a sense, however tenuous, of continuity and coherence. This, in turn, is related to a sense of identity. Memories may be painful, but Winton's characters cause themselves even more unhappiness by repressing memories; without memories, they seem unable even to feel. The boy in 'No Memory Comes' attempts to deal with the pain generated by memories and the reality of change by becoming drunk. This leads to him 'starting to feel dead' (p.19), a state in which there are 'no memories coming' (p.20) and in which the boy's tenuous sense of self is virtually obliterated.

Jerra Nilsam realises in 'Gravity' that, for all the difficulties of his relationship with his father and the sense of loss he feels following his father's death, being his father's son is crucial to his sense of identity. His knowledge and appreciation of this relationship is now completely dependent on memories: of his father's hands 'hairy with pollard' (p.29), or of his father teaching him to ride a bike. In 'Bay of Angels' Jerra sits with a friend close to the beach where he 'learnt to walk' (p.91), and where he promises himself he will bring his own son, Sam.

In 'Laps', Queenie also finds that her sense of identity is inseparable from events in her past, and that she is recognised by others for these events, too: 'I know who she is' asserts the man who guards the farm (p.85, 'Laps'). Irrespective of whether these memories are of a loving grandfather, or of being rejected by one's home town, they all intersect with each other and are integral to a person's personal history and identity.

Destroying the past

The value that the text places on memory providing connections to the past is reinforced by its critique of changes that erase signs of the past. This is particularly evident in 'Laps' and 'No Memory Comes'. Queenie is saddened to see her grandfather's farm now 'overgrazed and guttered...the hill showed signs of tree-felling' (p.85, 'Laps'). Her memories are of a past in which little changed for a hundred and fifty years, reflected in the house that 'seemed to have been dug into the granite flank of the hill' (p.82). That so much heritage can be rapidly destroyed by the actions of those who are insensitive to it is registered as a loss to the whole community in these narratives.

Typically, such changes are characterised as replacing beauty with ugliness, as in the development on the Scarborough beachfront – 'a rotten mess' Dot calls it (p.76) – or the 'ugly bones of the hotel tower' in 'No Memory Comes' (p.17). The stories represent such developments as bringing no real benefits to their communities, and as erasing older landscapes and cultures that are valuable in more than a merely economic sense.

The buoyancy of water

Key quotes

'He said these afternoons helped him stay afloat; it was like jettisoning cargo' (p.91, 'Bay of Angels').

'She'd had to jettison more than he had to stay afloat...' (p.98, 'The Strong One').

Most of the stories are set on or near the coast, a space that typically represents an opportunity for refuge and recovery. In 'Bay of Angels', Jerra suggests that: 'We always come back to water. When things happen' (p.93). In 'Laps', Queenie swims to recover her emotional as well as physical strength, and returns to the beach on what had been her grandfather's farm in order to reconcile herself to past losses and hurts.

Water is not an unfailing source of comfort in these stories, and Queenie finds that the beach also brings back distressing memories of 'where everything came aground' (p.86). However, on a metaphorical level, water offers a force, akin to a redeeming force, that helps the characters counteract the multiple weights of their lives: of memories, of past hurts and losses, of unhappiness and frustration in the present.

Key point

The capacity to float in water – to be buoyant – functions as a metaphor for emotional resilience. In this way, the text suggests that, despite the negative effects of traumatic experiences and daily struggles for survival, life always contains the possibility of solace and relief.

Rachel thinks of herself as having to 'jettison' aspects of her past 'in order to stay afloat' (p.98, 'The Strong One'), while Jerra's friend in 'Bay of Angels' finds that his afternoons with Jerra 'helped him stay afloat…like jettisoning cargo' (p.91). The metaphor is made literally true when they go for a swim in the bay, but the friend finds it tiring rather than relaxing, and at the end of the story he 'began to weep' (p.93). Here, although the water offers solace, it does not provide a cure; survival is one thing, but happiness, in these stories, is a far more ephemeral and elusive quality altogether.

Queenie in 'Laps' and the girl in 'The Water Was Dark...' both swim in order to feel better about themselves, but they do not have the same degree of self-knowledge. Queenie knows, as the narrative knows, that she is swimming to relieve herself of the weight of the past: 'she knew she could swim it all out of her' (p.87). Similarly, the girl's swimming prowess in 'The Water Was Dark...' is bound up with her attempt to gain control over her own destiny.

However, whereas Queenie wants to feel better, the girl desires not to feel anything, and this denial of feeling is represented as problematic. Although the girl swims strongly across the surface of the water, imagining that she is as unfeeling as a machine, the depth of the emotions she is trying to suppress is reflected – metaphorically – by the depth of the ocean beneath her. She feels 'young and strong and perfect' but the 'cold darkness' of the water suggests something more troubling (p.39). The girl is determined to become independent of her mother, but 'cold darkness' hints at loneliness and isolation in the wider world without the emotional connections and support, however difficult they may be to sustain, of family.

Negotiating gender roles

Minimum of Two explores the feelings of dislocation and lack of direction in life experienced by men who find that traditional male roles are not freely available to them. Male characters such as Jerra, Hart (in 'Holding') and Madigan (in 'Minimum of Two') struggle in domestic circumstances that are at odds with their expectations. For Hart and Madigan, the breakdowns in their marriages are devastating; it is not simply the lack of sexual relations that hurts them, but the loss of companionship and emotional support that has the most impact. Work can partially offset these losses, but eventually Madigan is 'so far behind schedule that it seemed hopeless' (p.57), while Hart becomes incapable of even going to work.

Jerra is far more successful than Hart and Madigan in adapting to new domestic arrangements, largely because of Rachel's support and commitment to the marriage. Although his despair in 'Forest Winter' and his affair (referred to in 'More') show that the responsibilities of being a father and husband do not always come easily to him, the stories depict Jerra's increasing contentment in these roles. Jerra may feel 'dowdy like women were supposed to feel dowdy' (p.45, 'Nilsam's Friend'), but his friend's observation that Jerra is a good father to Sam is supported by the narrative in several stories. In 'Laps', Cleve is also a good father, seemingly content to cook the breakfast and exchange 'Breakfast Banter' (p.78) with Dot.

Key point

Through depicting a range of responses to changing or fractured family structures, *Minimum of Two* reflects a broader social questioning of the role(s) of men in the home and the workplace that continues to the present day.

Private male spaces

Although these male characters demonstrate some flexibility with regard to gender roles, two of them retain a private, male space into which they retreat for solace at times of emotional hardship. Both Jerra and Madigan have a workshop/studio, an equivalent to the older male 'shed' updated to accommodate work as well as leisure pursuits. However, there is no similar private space afforded to female characters.

Combined with the stories' limited representations of the inner thoughts or feelings of women, this lack of an individualised female space suggests one of two things: that the women in the stories are incapable of reflection, or that they are emotionally resourceful enough to cope with the demands placed upon them. While the latter possibility represents women positively, this unbalanced allocation of space within the home reflects the persistence of older notions of masculinity into a period of flux and renegotiation of gender roles.

A sense of place versus the desire to travel

Many of the characters in these stories have a strong connection with the places where they live or have grown up. Invariably, these are located near bodies of water, such as the ocean or rivers. Characters who feel such an attachment to place include the boy in 'No Memory Comes', Queenie in 'Laps' and Jerra, especially in 'Bay of Angels'.

Yet a more pervasive quality in this collection is a restlessness, a desire to travel to another place or perhaps, as for Jerra's friend, simply to be on the move. Jerra has his own restless past, one that Rachel recalls as 'cruising up and down the coast in a Kombi' (p.100, 'The Strong One'). The characters' desire to travel may be expressed as a yearning to be somewhere other than their claustrophobic home environment, which the girl in 'The Water Was Dark...' certainly experiences, and Fat Maz increasingly feels in 'Distant Lands'. Or it may be a desperate need to travel to a place that can provide medical treatment or simply some respite and solace.

All of the journeys in these stories are marked by anxiety and tension. In 'More', the Nilsams' drive to the doctor's for Jerra to receive stitches is followed shortly afterwards by another trip when Sam appears to have swallowed rat poison. Although Sam is unharmed, the drives to and from the doctor's surgery reflect the lack of real direction or purpose in their lives. To gain a more supportive environment, Rachel decides they should go to Jerra's parents, and as she moves 'into top gear' (p.126) this drive takes on more positive implications. Jerra and Rachel's car trips to a chemist in 'Forest Winter' and to hospital in 'Blood and Water' are journeys motivated by life and death situations, filled with panic and feelings of helplessness. Even attaining the destination does not mean that their difficulties are over, and indeed in 'Blood and Water' the Nilsams' arrival at the hospital signals only the beginning of a far more traumatic 'journey'.

In 'Minimum of Two', Madigan hires a car with the intention of running over his wife's rapist, Blakey. Madigan is successful, yet the outcome he really desires – the restoration of his life as it was before Greta's rape – is not what he achieves. Instead, in destroying the lives of Blakey and his girlfriend, Madigan also destroys his own life; as an attempt to recover the past, this journey is a failure.

In contrast, the Cooksons travel back to Angelus in order for Queenie to resolve tensions from her and Cleve's past, and Queenie does gain some satisfaction from this trip. Like Madigan, Queenie arrives at the destination in a literal sense and this leads to a freshening in her mind of the conflicts of the past. At first, the Cooksons walk around Angelus 'without much sense of purpose or direction' (p.80). Later, Queenie is denied entry to the farm that used to belong to her family, which suggests the impossibility of ever completely returning to one's origins, or of recovering the innocence of childhood. Unlike Madigan, though, Queenie does become at least partially reconciled to past events, and accepts that the rest of this 'journey' will simply be 'a matter of time' (p.87).

Moments of revelation and acceptance

Many of these stories conclude on a note of uncertainty, or even of despair. However, more optimistically, they also suggest that even the most sceptical individuals are capable of experiencing a moment of heightened understanding or a glimpse of the other-worldly. In this way, the characters' struggle for survival and contentment is balanced by their capacity for acceptance and self-awareness.

Several stories conclude with the central character experiencing an insight into the true nature of their situation. Fat Maz in 'Distant Lands' seems to realise for the first time that the door to her parents' newsagency is not the means of confinement but an opening to freedom. Madigan experiences a less uplifting revelation when he realises that by murdering Blakey he has also destroyed his own life. Jerra's feeling of calm acceptance at the conclusion of 'Gravity' is less momentous, but it nevertheless marks a significant shift in Jerra's outlook. From this point, Jerra will be more capable of leaving the past behind and of bearing family responsibilities.

'Death Belongs To The Dead...' concludes with a revelatory moment that gestures towards the spiritual, and in so doing shares something of the philosophical and religious enquiry of the mediaeval Morality Play.

Sources of moral truth

'Death Belongs to the Dead...' may be interpreted as modern version of the mediaeval Morality Play, a theatrical form that was popular in the 1400s and early 1500s. These plays present a Christian view of human nature and morality, and often include God and the Devil as characters. In one of the most celebrated Morality Plays, *Everyman* (performed around 1500), the central character is called Everyman and is summoned by Death. Other characters in the play are Goods, Knowledge, Beauty and Strength, but Everyman discovers that the only one he can take with him is Good Deeds.[4]

Winton's story is very similar to a Morality Play. The central character is called The Man and although he initially tries to look away from Death he eventually discovers he cannot. Indeed, at the end of the story The Man looks directly 'into the Gentleman's face' (p.138) and accepts that such a distance – from other people, or from death – can only be illusory.

[4] See 'Morality Play' in J. A. Cuddon, *The Penguin Dictionary of Literary Terms and Literary Theory*, 3rd edition, Penguin, London, 1992, pp.555–6.

However, there are some significant departures from the Morality Play genre. Firstly, Death is not actually a character in Winton's story, but The Man identifies certain characters as 'the dead' (p.135). This reflects not so much a universal condition as The Man's own personal philosophy, his notion that he can project death onto other people but not onto himself.

A second difference from the Morality Play is that the story does not include God as a character. Thus, the story contains no embodiment of moral truth, no absolute reference point by which human beings can distinguish right behaviour from wrong. It is not that the story suggests that there is no God (an *atheistic* position), but that knowledge about the existence or non-existence of God is not available to the characters (an *agnostic* position). In such a scenario, it is up to human individuals to make moral choices based on their own experiences and their own apprehension of the roles of suffering and compassion in life.

The other-world within this world

Like 'Death Belongs to the Dead...', several other stories show characters gaining a glimpse of the other-worldly without unambiguously invoking the existence of a divine being. Clive's religious belief allows him to achieve a kind of inner peace that the sceptical Hart lacks, but the story suggests that family might just as effectively heal Hart's profound sense of loss. Hart dreams about Jan Genders's miscarriage before he even learns of her pregnancy; Hart feels as if he has received a message that is not of this world, though not necessarily from a God. He is incapable of communicating it to Clive or Jan and simply feels 'bad, sick...It scared him' (p.109).

In 'Blood and Water' Jerra repeats lines from a bedtime prayer to himself and exhorts 'Jesus Christ' not to 'fuck around with me' (p.150), but this does not mean that Sam and Rachel's survival is therefore a sign of the existence of God. Winton suggests that there is something spiritual about the birth process, but the prayer simply provides Jerra with a few words with which to conceptualise his experiences in the delivery room rather than the 'right' approach to such mysteries. In 'The Strong One', Jerra's feeling about Sean's death also suggests that Jerra can be touched by the other-worldly. Yet he, like most of Winton's characters, remains a sceptic throughout, preferring to accept that some things are simply mysterious without seeking further knowledge or explanation.

QUESTIONS & ANSWERS

This section focuses on your own analytical writing on the text, and gives you strategies for producing high quality responses in your coursework and exam essays.

In writing on a collection of short stories, your response will depend crucially on which stories you focus on. Try to balance detailed reference to two or three stories with your display of knowledge of the collection as a whole. Don't just discuss the stories individually as if they are completely isolated from each other, but move confidently between stories, showing connections between them as well as points of difference.

Essay writing – an overview

An essay on a literary work is a formal and serious piece of writing that presents your point of view on the text, usually in response to a given topic. Your 'point of view' in an essay is your interpretation of the meaning of the text's language, structure, characters, situations and events, supported by detailed analysis of textual evidence.

Analyse – don't summarise

In your essays it is important to avoid simply summarising what happens in a text:

- A **summary** is a description or paraphrase (retelling in different words) of the characters and events. For example: 'Macbeth has a horrifying vision of a dagger dripping with blood before he goes to murder King Duncan'.
- An **analysis** is an explanation of the real meaning or significance that lies 'beneath' the text's words (and images, for a film). For example: 'Macbeth's vision of a bloody dagger shows how deeply uneasy he is about the violent act he is contemplating – as well as his sense that supernatural forces are impelling him to act'.

A limited amount of summary is sometimes necessary to let your reader know which part of the text you wish to discuss. However, always keep this to a minimum and follow it immediately with your analysis (explanation) of what this part of the text is really telling us.

Plan your essay

Carefully plan your essay so that you have a clear idea of what you are going to say. The plan ensures that your ideas flow logically, that your argument remains consistent and that you stay on the topic. An essay plan should be a list of **brief dot points** – no more than half a page.

- Include your central argument or main contention – a concise statement (usually in a single sentence) of your overall response to the topic. See 'Analysing a sample topic' for guidelines on how to formulate a main contention.
- Write three or four dot points for each paragraph indicating the main idea and evidence/examples from the text. Note that in your essay you will need to *expand* on these points and *analyse* the evidence.

Structure your essay

An essay is a complete, self-contained piece of writing. It has a clear beginning (the introduction), middle (several body paragraphs) and end (the last paragraph or conclusion). It must also have a central argument that runs throughout, linking each paragraph to form a coherent whole.

The introduction establishes your overall response to the topic. It includes your main contention and outlines the main evidence you will refer to in the course of the essay. Write your introduction *after* you have done a plan and *before* you write the rest of the essay.

The body paragraphs argue your case – they present evidence from the text and explain how this evidence supports your argument. Each body paragraph needs:

- a strong **topic sentence** (usually the first sentence) that states the main point being made in the paragraph
- **evidence** from the text, including some brief quotations

- **analysis** of the textual evidence explaining its significance and **explanation** of how it supports your argument
- **links back to the topic** in one or more statements, usually towards the end of the paragraph.

Connect the body paragraphs so that your discussion flows smoothly. Use some linking words and phrases like 'similarly' and 'on the other hand', though don't start every paragraph like this. Another strategy is to use a significant word from the last sentence of one paragraph in the first sentence of the next.

Use key terms from the topic – or synonyms for them – throughout, so the relevance of your discussion to the topic is always clear.

The conclusion ties everything together and finishes the essay. It includes strong statements that emphasise your central argument and provide a clear response to the topic.

Avoid simply restating the points made earlier in the essay – this will end on a very flat note and imply that you have run out of ideas and vocabulary. The conclusion is meant to be a logical extension of what you have written, not just a repetition or summary. Writing an effective conclusion can be a challenge. Try using these tips:

- Start by linking back to the final sentence of the second-last paragraph – this helps your writing to 'flow', rather than just leaping back to your main contention straight away.
- Use synonyms and expressions with equivalent meanings to vary your vocabulary. This allows you to reinforce your line of argument without being repetitive.
- When planning your essay, think of one or two broad statements or observations about the text's wider meaning. These should be related to the topic and your overall argument. Keep them for the conclusion, since they will give you something 'new' to say but still follow logically from your discussion. The introduction will be focused on the topic, but the conclusion can present a wider view of the text.

Essay topics

1. How do images of the natural world reflect the emotional lives of Winton's characters?

2. Hart says: "I am not coping". Why do the male characters struggle to cope?

3. 'Winton's male characters find a sense of purpose in life only when they can perform maternal, nurturing roles.' Discuss.

4. "Something's happening for me, Jerra. I'm getting somewhere."

   'The female characters in *Minimum of Two* look to the future more positively than their male counterparts.' Do you agree?

5. "Don't be bitter, be better."

   'The characters' bitter feelings about their pasts stop them living better lives.' Discuss.

6. "There was a hole in him. Something was lost."

   '*Minimum of Two* shows that the loss of others is as bewildering and painful as if part of oneself is lost.' Discuss.

7. "Nilsam was a father. He was a husband. He was a son."

   'Winton shows that family relationships are crucial to our sense of identity.' Discuss.

8. 'Winton suggests that ordinary life can always produce miracles.' Discuss.

9. "He had a son to look after, and a wife to consider."

   'Winton's stories suggest that there are more roles available to men than simply that of the breadwinner.' Discuss.

10. "Jerra seemed to bear weights from the past as though they were treasures he had to take with him."

    '*Minimum of Two* shows that although the past is important it is less important than the present and the future.' Do you agree?

Analysing a sample topic

"There was a hole in him. Something was lost."
'*Minimum of Two* shows that the loss of others is as bewildering and painful as if part of oneself is lost.' Discuss.

This question focuses on the theme of loss in the stories and the way in which the characters internalise loss. This reflects the importance of certain individuals (such as fathers) and relationships to one's own sense of self, and also the tendency of some characters to feel excessive self-pity. This second, more critical perspective, allows for some pressure to be placed on the contention; it suggests that it is not loss as such that causes pain, but a lack of emotional or spiritual resources, such as religious faith or a sense of purpose in life.

Evidence

The quotation that precedes the contention clearly identifies Jerra as one who experiences loss, in particular the loss of his father as explored in 'Gravity'. Other characters who experience loss as if something inside their own bodies has been removed are:

- The boy in 'No Memory Comes': experiences the loss of his father, and then the end of high school means the loss of childhood certainties; he 'feels a hole open in him' (p.17).
- Madigan in 'Minimum of Two': experiences the loss of intimacy in his marriage; his body 'began to feel as though something had been hacked out of it' (p.57).
- Hart in 'Holding': has lost his wife and wonders 'whether he mightn't have lost himself as well' (p.113); this makes explicit the connection between the loss of a relationship and the loss of identity.

Relating evidence to the topic

These examples of characters experiencing loss must be related to the contention, in particular to its key terms 'bewildering' and 'painful'. A good quotation to use here is the description of Jerra's feeling on the anniversary of his father's death as 'full of ghostly associations like... amputees' (p.25, 'Gravity'). Jerra's bewilderment is evident: he feels haunted, as if he is still in possession of something (his relationship with his father) which he knows no longer exists.

Other characters show bewilderment through unusual, antisocial behaviour. Hart stops working and seems unable to communicate; Madigan acts completely irrationally, imagining that murdering his wife's rapist will restore his marriage.

That loss is painful is indicated by the boy's self-inflicted wound in 'No Memory Comes'. The beer can in the beach house is a relic from the past when the boy's father was part of his life; by trying to open it the boy achieves only 'the cold shock of steel in his groin' (p.20). An important point to make if you wish to disagree with the contention is that this is pain the boy causes himself. That is, you could argue that it is the way he responds to loss – of his father and even of his friendship in its original form – rather than the loss itself that causes bewilderment and pain.

Making an argument

The simplest argument is one that agrees with the contention. You would use the evidence to show how the characters experience loss as a loss of/inside oneself. Each paragraph could deal with one story or character, emphasising the similarities between characters' experiences and responses.

A more complex argument might be formed by placing pressure on the contention and suggesting that it is a feature of the characters' personalities that causes them to experience loss in this way. Interestingly, each of the characters referred to above under 'evidence' is male; a contrast could be made with Queenie Cookson in 'Laps', who experiences the past not in terms of loss but as a weight to be shed. Thus, the male characters might internalise loss as a result of their inability to articulate their emotions; their bewilderment and pain might not be something loss does to them, but rather something they do to themselves.

Conclusion

The conclusion must draw together the evidence you have utilised and relate it clearly to the terms of the topic. Keep using the key terms 'bewilderment', 'pain/painful' and 'loss' to make these connections.

Additionally, the conclusion must state succinctly the argument you are presenting – your 'take' on the contention. If you agree with the contention, you might conclude that Winton's representation of loss as a loss of part of oneself shows the strength of close relationships and their importance to our sense of identity. Or, if you argue that experiencing loss in this way is due to an emotional response that exacerbates the pain of loss, you could conclude that Winton thereby demonstrates the importance of communication and of expressing our feelings to others.

SAMPLE ANSWER

"It's just a beach. Just a place."

'Winton's stories demonstrate that we can never go back to the past.' Discuss.

Through the stories in *Minimum of Two,* Winton explores the complex relationships that individuals have with their pasts, relationships that are sustained through the medium of memory. For many of the characters, memories are intensely ambivalent: the past is a source of pain, yet it is simultaneously almost irresistibly attractive, tempting some characters to live more in their memories than in the present. Nostalgia is prevalent throughout this collection: a longing to return to the past that frequently compounds the characters' problems. However, Winton does not imply that the past must therefore be forgotten, or that it should have no place in our emotional and imaginative lives. On the contrary, Winton shows that past experiences are crucial sources of meaning and continuity, but they must always be balanced with the needs and opportunities of the present moment.

The most overt way in which Winton represents characters seeking to return to the past is through a physical journey to a significant place from the past – especially a place treasured in childhood. Queenie Cookson in 'Laps' undertakes the most deliberate of these trips into the past. She invests the town in which she grew up, Angelus, with great significance, taking her husband and daughter there one weekend specifically to revisit the sites of her most intense experiences, both traumatic and pleasurable. Foremost among these places is the beach on what had been her grandfather's property. For Queenie, this beach is almost unbearably charged with meaning. Her husband, Cleve, attempts to divest the beach of some of this emotional weight, saying: 'it's just a beach. Just a place'. Yet its significance for Queenie is not actually as a means of returning to the past, which she acknowledges is neither possible nor desirable. Rather, it is a place where she may measure how far she has moved on in her life;

it also allows Queenie to recognise the extent to which she remains too emotionally attached to past events and feelings.

In other stories, journeys to important places in the characters' lives broaden the scope of this metaphor for the impossibility of returning to the past. Jerra Nilsam's nostalgic disposition is a source of frustration for his wife, Rachel, in 'The Strong One'. When they walk past one of Jerra's old camping sites, Rachel reads his expression as a sign that 'the past had hold of him'. She rejects his tendency to inhabit the past through his memories, and Jerra's evident struggle to adjust to their present situation – the need to care for their son and Rachel's desire to gain a university qualification – validates Rachel's perspective.

Yet Jerra's obsession with the past has its strengths as well as its weaknesses, as 'Bay of Angels' suggests. The memories and associations of the beach on which Jerra 'learnt to walk' are clearly rich sources of meaning and coherence in his life. Here, Winton suggests that, although returning to the past is impossible, it may be tremendously fulfilling to remain in touch with aspects of it.

A much more desperate, and ultimately self-destructive, attempt to recover a past state of being is played out in 'Minimum of Two', in which Madigan attempts to kill his wife's rapist in order to restore the intimacy of his marriage. He asks himself, 'when do I get back everything that once belonged to me, for Chrissake?', refusing to accept that such a restoration of the past is impossible. Like Queenie and Jerra, Madigan revisits important sites from the past, such as the car park where Greta had been raped and 'an Italian place' they had frequented in the early years of their marriage. These places only serve to remind Madigan of how much has changed, so he sets out to eradicate the cause of this change, as if this will take Greta and him back to their former selves. Of course, the murder of Blakey only precipitates further momentous changes in Madigan's life, signalling that the attempt to go back to the past may itself place past circumstances even further out of reach.

The idea of returning to the past is explored repeatedly in *Minimum of Two* by a journey. Although the physical destination may be arrived at, Winton always demonstrates that the temporal destination is not achievable. Jerra and Queenie accept this, suggesting that a balance may be reached whereby the past might be longed for but can also be incorporated into our sense of self, giving continuity and meaning to life. Madigan, though, speaks for the opposite of this psychological state, in which the strong desire for a past situation leads to an insane attempt to recover it. Such an endeavour, Winton makes clear, is always doomed: the past is *past*, and between it and the present is a gap that, while perhaps measurable in a few months or years, must always remain impossible to traverse.

REFERENCES & READING

Text

Winton, Tim, *Minimum of Two*, Penguin, Ringwood, 1998. (First published by McPhee Gribble, 1987.)

Newspaper articles

Daley, Paul, 'Tim Winton dirt smart', *The Age*, 26 May 2002, The Culture p.1.

Steger, Jason, 'A big night in for Miles Franklin winner', *The Age*, 14 June 2002, p.1.

Winton, Tim, 'Our reef, my belief', *The Weekend Australian*, 30 November-1 December 2002, p.21.

Film and video

Bennett, Geoffrey (director), *The Edge of the World*, Film Australia, 1998.

This documentary about Tim Winton features the author and is set in the Kimberley region of Western Australia. Available on DVD; contact the National Film & Sound Archive (nfsa.gov.au) for details.

Website

https://www.nfsa.gov.au/collection/curated/edge-world

These excellent notes are designed to accompany the film *The Edge of the World* but can be read independently of it. They include biographical details and analysis of the Western Australian context and central concerns in Winton's writing, for example, isolation, displacement, masculinity and children – all relevant to *Minimum of Two*.